Paint the City Red

by

Lee A. Pitts

ISBN-13: 978-0-9964192-0-8
ISBN-10: 0-9964192-0-9

Paint the City Red© 2015 by Lee A. Pitts

www.LeeAPitts.com

Library of Congress Cataloging-in-Publication Data
Pitts, Lee A
Paint the City Red: a novel/by Lee A. Pitts

Published in the United States of America by UrbanRoom, LLC, New York, NY

This book is a work of fiction. Names, characters, and incidents included are done so with the expressed consent of those mentioned.

Paint the City Red   by Lee A. Pitts

CONTENTS

PROLOGUE

New Year's Eve

"It's been a long year and a half since we started this case. Every time we turn around there's been one roadblock after another getting in our way. But I think we may have a break in the case this time. If the information that we have turns out to be true, there's gonna be a hit going down tonight, fellas," FBI Agent Sam Bauer said to the other agents as they are staked out in a second floor apartment located in the three-story apartment building; across the street from Black Roses Lounge.

"Haze just showed up," Agent John Mackey said as the rest of the agents began to watch Haze greet people and take a few pictures on the red carpet before entering the lounge.

The lyrics from the song, "Never Surrender" were blasting through the speakers inside the Black Roses Lounge. Conveniently located on 47th Avenue and Vernon Boulevard in Long Island City, Queens, the lounge is the brand new late-night hangout for the major league street crew in the borough. It's also the main focus of the FBI's current surveillance operation.

It's New Year's Eve and it's about forty-five minutes before the ball drops; the lounge is packed with people. Bottles of Dom Perignon, Patron and Hennessy sit in black and gold buckets filled with ice on every table throughout the lounge. Heavy cigar smoke lingers in the air as sexy women along with a who's who list of ballplayers, celebrities, rappers, close friends and business associates of King take up every inch of vacant space in the lounge. The joint is on point and everyone is ready to bring the New Year in with a bang while celebrating the grand opening of the lounge. King is the owner of Black Roses Lounge; he originally came up with the concept as a chill spot for him and his crew as a safe haven when they were off the clock of the streets.

Walking through the front door, the appearance of the lounge has a modern and welcoming feel to it. LED ceiling panel lights in red, gold and black with custom-made decorations and mirrored framing cover the ceiling throughout the majority of the lounge. It has a spacious L-shaped bar area, with a black marble granite counter top. Three bartenders and six waitresses work the main area and more than one hundred different liquors and wines align the back wall of the bar. Two 65-inch 4K-Ultra flat screen TVs hang from the ceiling above the bar; visible from any seat in the lounge. There's also a nice sized VIP area were the lighting from the LED star ceiling panel is dimmer than the rest of the lounge, giving it a more subtle and relaxing feel. Two large classical paintings of the Roman Empire in rose gold picture frames hang on the black walls of the VIP area above four long, red leather Louis Vuitton sofas. Two long, rectangular-shaped black wooden tables custom-made by Versace are placed in the middle of the VIP room. Each holds four buckets filled with ice and complimentary champagne bottles. Those on the VIP list mingle with the rest of the partygoers where the music meets the dance floor. It's a forty-foot by forty-foot hardwood section toward the back of the lounge and the lighting is a little brighter than the rest of the lounge so that those on the dance floor can see one another a little better. To add a bit of home and camaraderie to the joint, the walls are painted black and red with pictures of King and his crew partying in different countries that they have been to; right beside those pictures are autographed photos of ballplayers and rappers that made it out of Queensbridge, some of which are in attendance for the opening. The picture hall of fame was King's way of saying, *don't forget where you came from or where you're going.*

To the left of the bar is a red wall; a focal point that King dedicated to the fallen soldiers from his crew who had died on the streets. Some crews pour out liquor or get tattoos in homage to soldiers that have earned their stripes, but King preferred to show his respect through photos for all to see eternally. Their pictures were tastefully hung on the wall in rose gold picture frames side by side. The words centered above the pictures in gold letters solidified his feelings for each of them: *Gone But Never Forgotten.*

The atmosphere in the lounge begins to heighten and it is clear that everyone is having a good time. Haze – the manager of the lounge and the crew's second in charge – is in the back office trying to get details from Nando Sanchez about a storage facility of theirs which was robbed earlier in the morning. It was a hard hit for the crew; ten million dollars of dope, four million dollars of cocaine and five million dollars of Methamphetamine pills had been taken and Haze wanted explanations; quick, fast and in a hurry.

"UN...FUCKIN'...BELIEVABLE!" Haze said, leaning back in his leather chair and staring at Nando Sanchez.

Nando's Spanish accent adds a sense of urgency and flavor as he speaks; he knows the urgency of the situation. "I have no idea how they got the drop on us. My men dropped off the first part of the shipment at your warehouse and then headed to my location, which nobody knows about, to drop off the rest. I don't think that any of my men are to blame for this. It had to be a set up because they were rushed as soon as they got there. They were sitting ducks for an ambush. I lost some really loyal soldiers this morning; four of my men were killed. Three motherfuckers in ski masks with M16s got the jump on them, from what I'm told," he lets out a slight sigh and shakes his head toward Haze. "There's a snake in your crew, my man. You and King better find out who it is, and quick before it happens again and your own men start dropping like flies," Nando stated, observing Haze and his reaction.

Hiding his anger and showing no emotion, Haze gets up from his custom-made Hermes Oak wood desk and walks over to his closet. Known for his impeccable taste in fashion, Haze is recognized as the most stylish dresser in the crew. As he opens the doors of his custom-made Hermes wooden closet, the latest top of-the-line designer dress shirts, blazers, sweaters and jeans hang from the rod.

A dozen sneakers by Balenciaga, Gucci and Retro Jordan's take up the top self; as a dozen Tom Ford hard-bottom shoes in different colors and styles are placed side by side at the bottom of the closet. Before speaking, Haze scans through the section which is the left side of the closet where the dress shirts are, and he pulls out and puts on a black and red, silk Versace button-down shirt from his collection. As the silk hits his back a sense of composure comes over him, calming him down from what he just heard.

"Well, you don't have to worry about that. King and I are going to find out who was behind it. I give you my word!" he said before turning back and looking at Nando with a smile on his face. "And once we do, there will be hell to pay; their families will be erased right along with them," he assured Nando as he buttoned up his shirt and admired the way he looked in the full-length, stand-alone wood mirror in the corner.

"I know y'all will. I have faith in that," Nando replied, getting up from his chair and putting on his blue blazer.

"What a way to end the year, huh? I hope losing that much money isn't an omen," Haze said, staring in the mirror at the scar across the right cheek of his face. He

11

shook his head before pulling out a Lano Estate cigar. "But let's forget about that right now; it's New Year's Eve and there are a lot of people out there partying and enjoying themselves and King should be here any minute. So let's go have a good time tonight and get fucked up like how y'all do in Mexico. We'll take care of everything tomorrow," he said, putting his arm around Nando as they both laughed and walked out of the office.

"It's show time!" Agent Mackey said to the other agents in the apartment. They all watched on the surveillance monitor as a beige Maserati blasting the song, "No Ordinary Love" pulled up and parked in front of Black Roses Lounge.

Hopping out the driver's side wearing a beige sport's coat over a black, silk Versace shirt, black jeans and tan construction Timbs is Aaron "King" Johnson. The twenty-nine year old has become a multi-millionaire from running the biggest drug empire in Queens. Not only does he control the streets, but he also has half a dozen businesses that he owns as to keep the legit money flowing; all of which he put into play in a little over a year and a half. His beautiful fiancé, Kia, steps out of the passenger side. She turns heads in a pair of black, Tom Ford Nappa leather laced-up pumps, and a cream-colored short cut

Givenchy dress that shows off her long legs and amazing curves.

We're finally gonna get you, you son of a bitch, Agent Bauer said to himself as he watched King and Kia walk into the lounge.

As they enter, all eyes are on them as they make their way through and begin greeting everybody that came to celebrate the New Year and the grand opening. Haze, coming from around the bar, walks up to King, hugs him and gives him a bottle of Dom Perignon. The two men fist bump and Haze instructs the DJ to turn off the music. Heads turn in their direction and conversations begin to cease as Haze begins to speak.

"Everybody…please let me have your attention. I want to make a toast, so will everyone lift your bottles and glasses and let's toast to the newly-engaged couple: King and Kia. Congratulations to you both," Haze says as the lounge erupts in cheers and clapping that can be heard down the block.

The sound of the Heckler & Koch MP-5N sub machine gun being cocked back echoes inside the black S-Class Benz parked across the street from the lounge. Opening the passenger side door, dressed in all black, he hears the loud chant of the countdown taking place from inside the lounge and his adrenaline starts pumping.

"5, 4, 3, 2, 1."

"HAPPY NEW YEAR"

CHAPTER 1

"From that moment on, he was a big brother to
King."

A year and a half earlier

Thursday, July 21
Queens, New York

It's ninety degrees and another hot summer day in
the notoriously known, Queensbridge Housing Projects; the
biggest housing projects in the world. Opened in 1939, it
has ninety-six buildings sitting on six city blocks and
divided into two sides; North – the 40th side, and South –
the 41st side. Although it is crime-ridden, it is also the
birthplace of some of the most successful rappers, NBA
players, authors, film producers and many other successful
professionals; proving that growing up in the hood does not
mean you are limited to it. But then there's the dark side of
Queensbridge, just like any other housing project or bad
neighborhood throughout America. Murder, drugs, gangs,
prostitution, and anything else you can name go on there.

Along with its reputation for producing famous people, it is also the birthplace of a gangsta the streets of Queens and New York will forever remember: Aaron Johnson, aka, King.

Aaron Johnson was born on September 24, in New York Hospital in Manhattan, New York. Raised by both of his parents in the Queensbridge Housing Projects; his mother, Maria Johnson, was a nurse at Mount Sinai Hospital, and his father Chris Johnson, was an elevator mechanic. Growing up on the 41st side of 12th Street and being their only child, King was spoiled rotten by his parents. Chris and Maria bought him anything he wanted. He wasn't raised like the majority of the kids in the projects who came from unstable households. In most cases, those kids had parents who were on drugs or had fathers who had abandoned them either by choice or by death or incarceration. King was blessed with options in life to be successful because of his parents; but for some reason, he was fascinated with the street life – the drug dealers, money, cars, jewelry, women and especially the violence. Everything his parents tried to shield him from, he seemed drawn to.

Growing up and ignoring his parents' wishes for him to stay out of the streets and away from hanging with the wrong people, King would get in all kinds of trouble and eventually ended up doing six months on Rikers Island at the age of sixteen for a robbery he and his friend, Gotti, committed.

Doing the six months at Rikers only made King more of a true soldier to the streets. What he learned on the streets and from surviving in jail, King began to feel invincible, which only led to more problems, causing him to do time up north in State prison. The time he did there was the repercussion of him shooting a well-known stick-up kid named Spyda from Far Rockaway, Queens. Spyda had tried to rob King for his chain on the 4th of July, on 40th Avenue while King was walking to his car after leaving Monte's Lounge. King was already on point because he had gotten word that Spyda was in the hood driving around in a black Infiniti. Because of his reputation for sticking people up, King made sure he kept a look out for Spyda, so he didn't catch King by surprise.

Dressed in all black, and hiding down in the building's cellar on the passenger side of King's car, Spyda tried to creep as he saw King approaching his car. What Spyda didn't know at the time was that King already had his gun out and his finger on the trigger as he walked across the street towards his car. As soon as King saw someone creeping up the cellar ramp, he knew what was about to go down. He decided to shoot first and ask questions later. He shot Spyda in the stomach without thinking twice and then he got in his car and drove off. Spyda survived the shooting, but he was arrested on a gun charge when the police found him. So, like all cowards do, instead of taking the charge, he took the easy way out and snitched on King. King was arrested a month later for the shooting and sentenced to eight years after Spyda testified against him in court.

During his seven years up north, King read any and everything he could get his hands on. Strategy, business and marketing, and self-help books were his favorites. His muscular physique comes from the 1000 push-ups and sit-ups he would do on a daily basis during the seven years he was locked up. In every prison he was shipped to during that time, the women COs loved him and the male COs hated him. He got into plenty of fights with the male COs and other inmates, resulting in numerous trips to the box. Throughout the years in jail, King learned a lot from the older inmates; most of whom where lifers. All the insight and knowledge he learned from them just prepared him to become a more elusive, ruthless and smarter criminal when he got back out. He was at the top of his game before going in; but street smarts coupled with book smarts made him more of a threat to anyone in his path.

It's 2:30 in the afternoon, and twenty-seven-year-old King sits on the bench in front of 41-07 on the 41st side of 12th Street wearing a white Louis Vuitton t-shirt and beige cargo shorts with the black Foamposites on his feet. Both charismatic and fearless, standing 6'0" and weighing a stocky two hundred and thirty pounds, the brown-skinned, half-Black and half Puerto Rican is known and respected throughout Queens for his murder game and his hustler's ambition. Always with a fresh taper that highlights his three-sixty waves, King keeps a clean-shaven face and his thin goatee neatly trimmed. He has the same facial features as his father; a flat nose and down turned hazel eyes.

Even though he's one of the most treacherous gangstas to ever walk the streets of Queens, he's loved by the people of his neighborhood because of his kind heart, and approachable and engaging attitude. Besides terrorizing the streets, incompetent drug dealers and competing street crews, King contributes to his community enormously. He sponsors summer basketball tournaments for kids, turkey drives for Thanksgiving, and toy drives for Christmas. The Jacob Riis Community Center awarded him an Outstanding

Citizen Award for his contributions in the Queensbridge neighborhood over the years.

Watching a couple of kids playing basketball and old ladies sitting at the card tables gossiping, King waits for one of his comrades, Flush, to come downstairs. They made plans to go to 5th Avenue in Manhattan to buy clothes for Mac's 40th birthday party later on that night at Club Mansions located in the Chelsea District of Manhattan.

Tyler Hampton, aka Mac, is one of the major dope dealers on the streets of New York City. He took over the dope game in Queens ten years ago when his Uncle OG Zel blew trial and got life after being charged with counts of attempted murder of police officers at the South Street Seaport. Mac is known as the original fly gangsta of Queens. The dark skinned, 6'4" and two hundred and fifty pound ex-football player has been grooming King to one day replace him and run all of Queens and then hopefully all of New York City. Mac watched King grow up and he even coached him when he played on his basketball team in the Queensbridge summer tournaments. Mac took a liking to King and took him under his wing after King showed what he was made of by holding Mac down and putting his own life on the line for him a little over a year ago after he got out of the joint.

That day, Mac was in a shootout on 21st Street by himself with three dudes from Harlem who were paid to kill him. The hit was scheduled as payback for Mac having a stick-up kid named Benny killed for robbing his gambling spot in the Bronx. Benny was the son of Harlem drug kingpin, Butch Reed, and the kingpin wanted revenge for his son. When the hit went down, King was in the bedroom of his first floor apartment in building 41-05 on 12th Street when he heard gun shots ringing off. He looked out his window when he heard the shots and he saw Mac banging at three dudes dressed in all-black. King had looked up to Mac while growing up and he had heard all the stories about Mac while he was up north. He could see that Mac was outnumbered and he couldn't let him go out like that alone.

He knew that having Mac as an ally to him instead of an enemy would only help him on his rise in the streets. King grabbed his gun and hopped out of his bedroom window and started banging at the Harlem dudes right along with Mac like partners in a shootout. King's bullets hit one of them in the leg, killed another one and made the third gunmen run off toward Queens Plaza. Mac was stunned and amazed by what King had done for him. Hearing the police sirens in the distance, Mac hopped in his

21

Benz truck, told King to get in with him, and they sped off. From that moment on, Mac was a big brother to King; teaching him the dope and coke game.

Watching as Flush walks out of the building wearing his signature style Versace velour tracksuit, King gets up, shaking his head as Flush approaches with an irritated look on his face.

"Damn nigga, you got me out here waiting; you said you were getting ready when I called you," King said as he gives him a pound and a hug.

"My bad, I was recounting my money. I think my bitch took like two racks from me. I know I ain't spend it or gamble it away."

King shakes his head and lets out a slight laugh. "Shorty's a dime, but I told you she was a grimy broad and everybody and their father done fucked her, my nigga. You can't trust shit she says or does and you're playing yourself for even wifing her up," King told Flush as they walk toward 21st Street. "What's good, fam," King said, answering his phone. "Aight, me and Flush on 21st Street waiting for y'all," he ended his phone conversation as quickly as it started. "That was Haze; he's with Mel and Tone. They'll be here in five minutes," he said to Flush as they waited by his black S-class Benz on 21st Street.

King's crew consist of five members

Aaron Johnson, aka King. The twenty-seven year old is the mastermind and leader of the crew. He runs a tight ship and is well known for his ruthlessness. Any drug from dope, coke and weed sold on the 41st side of Queensbridge comes from him.

Darren Hall, aka Haze, is the crew's second in charge. Standing 6'3" and brown skinned with a muscular physique and an arrogant attitude, the twenty-seven year old handles the money and the product. He is also King's right-hand man.

Jason Rush, aka Flush, is the smallest person out of everyone. He stands 5'5" with a bronze-colored skin tone, he is short and skinny with a big head and wide eyes. Flush is a non-intimidating looking person on the surface; but just like his father, Heat, he loves busting his gun. The twenty-six year old is in charge of the workers on the street and recruiting of new workers. He's also like a little brother to King.

James Coleman, aka Mel, is the short and chubby funny man of the crew. He always makes everyone laugh, but he's about his business when it comes to the streets. 5'7" with a beige-colored skin tone, the twenty-six year old was the last member to join King and his crew. He's a wild

23

Haitian with a quick temper; that's why King put him down with his team. Mel is in charge of the re-ups and the drop offs of the product.

Anthony Harper, aka Tone, is the muscle of the crew along with King. He has that dark chocolate skin that women love and is bald headed. Standing 6'4" and a husky three hundred pounds, Tone is the type of person that even the toughest people won't fight. The twenty-nine year old is the oldest out of everybody and was the first member inducted in the crew. He and King were the first two out of everyone to start hustling in the streets and putting in work.

After meeting up on 21st Street, King and his crew hit up the Versace, Gucci and Louis Vuitton stores on 5th Avenue. By the end of the day, they had dropped twenty racks on clothes and sneakers to wear to Mac's party later on in the night. After that, they headed out to King's condo located in Long Island City, Queens. The rebuilt neighborhood had condos and skyscrapers mixed in with restaurants, stores and playgrounds for the kids. It's like a mini city within a city. Mac gave King the condo as a birthday gift a year ago. The spacious two-bedroom condo is on the 20th floor and overlooks the East river, with a view of Roosevelt Island and Manhattan.

Entering the apartment, everyone could smell the freshly baked lasagna, chicken cutlets, spaghetti and meatballs, and garlic bread. Kia, King's girlfriend, made the big meal for him and the fellas knowing that they were all stopping by. She was always pampering her man and the crew knew he was a lucky man to have a woman like her by his side.

Kia has a joyous smile that can brighten up the darkest room, and a charming personality you are easily attracted to. She's twenty-seven; half Black and half Puerto Rican, 5'3" with a caramel skin tone and long black and brownish naturally thick wavy hair. She wears little to no makeup and a straight nose and full lips complement her immaculate oval-shaped face. And last, but not least, Kia has the curvaceous body of a video model which only adds to her sex appeal. Tahkia Cruz and King have been together for ten years and have a five-year-old daughter named Nicole. Kia has been there for King through thick and thin. She's a real ride or die chick. From the death of his parents, being on the run with him, and being by his side for the whole seven-year bid, they have a bond that nobody can break. She even went against her parents' wishes and kept seeing King while he was locked up after they told her not to and she gave birth to Nicole when they told her to get an abortion. She became a successful business woman through the years; owning two hair salons and starting her own fashion magazine. She never lost sight of her goals, even while helping King hold down his.

"Where is my baby girl Nicole at?" Tone asked Kia as he gives her a hug.

"She's in her room watching the baseball game," she replied, taking the foil tops off of the trays of food.

"Nicole, your uncles are here!" King yelled out.

Nicole's face lights up with a big smile as she comes running into the living room and sees all of her uncles in the living room. One by one she gives each of them a big hug and a kiss. She knows they all consider her to be a princess and she takes advantage of her royalty every chance that she can. Nicole York Cruz was born on August 25, at 8:15 in the morning at New York Hospital. She weighed eight pounds and four ounces at birth. King was up north when Nicole was born, but his crew was there for the birth and took care of Kia while he was locked up. That kept him at ease for the seven years he was away and it formed a bond between Nicole and the members of the crew that she grew to know as her uncles. The adorable five year old resembles both of her parents. From the flat nose and down turned hazel eyes of her father, to her mother's oval-shaped face and caramel skin tone, and black and brown thick hair down her back. She also has an even mix of both of her parents' determination and charming personalities. King spoils Nicole just like his parents did to him. He buys her whatever she wants and takes her wherever she wants to go. Money is not an issue when it comes to his babygirl; and she and her mother both know it.

"Hann, this is from all of your uncles," Flush said, handing her a Gucci sneaker box.

Her eyes widen and a smile stretches across her face as she opens the box. "These are nice," she says pulling the beige and white Gucci sneakers out of the box. "I'mma wear these on my birthday; thank you."

"The food is ready, so y'all can help yourselves," King said as he fixed his own plate.

After eating, watching the Yankee game, and listening to Tone tell humorous and embarrassing stories to Nicole about her parents and her uncles, the fellas headed home to get ready for the party and King starts to get ready as well.

This Versace belt is fire, King says to himself; standing in the bedroom in front of the full-length mirror. While getting dressed, he hears his phone ringing and Mac's name appears on the screen.

"What's good, OG," King asked.

"Tonight…it's gonna be a movie. You already know how it's going down."

"I know, fam…I'm getting ready now. What time you showing up?"

"About 11:00 on the dot, my nigga. I'm bringing the ghost out too. I just bought it today; the all-white joint."

"Yeah, niggas is gonna be sick 'cause we rented some drop-top Ferraris in different colors for the rest of the crew; you know how we play."

Mac laughed. "I know, pull up by 11:00; aight."

"No doubt," King replied, hanging up the phone as he sees Kia standing in the doorway with an annoyed look on her face. That's one of the things that turned King on about her; even when she's mad, she still looked sexy to him.

"Go head," she said, staring at her man standing in front of the mirror. He looked good dressed in a creamed-colored Versace short-sleeve dress shirt with a matching bucket hat, beige pants, and cream-colored Versace sneakers and belt. "What…are you planning on sliding off with something after the party?" she asked, standing in the doorway of the bedroom. He could hear her question, but his eyes were fixated on the pair of pink booty shorts hugging her 40-inch ass and the tight, pink belly shirt that showed off her flat stomach.

"Why you come in here dressed like that? You making my dick hard," he said, putting on his gold Rolex watch and gold Cuban link chain with the iced-out Jesus head. "But now that I think about it, you probably are doing that shit on purpose trying to distract me."

With a smile on her face, Kia walks up behind him and hugs him. She inhales the fresh scent of Tom Ford cologne as she kisses him on the neck and rests her head on his shoulder. "I don't have to distract you, those hoodrats out there don't have anything on me and we both know it," she gives him a wink and plops down on the bed. "Bring some breakfast home with you when you come back," she said.

"And bring some ice cream from Bella's," Nicole screams out, running into the bedroom and hugging her father's leg.

Picking her up and kissing her on the forehead, King responds, "Bella's is closed. I'll bring some from the diner, babygirl."

"You're not going to forget are you daddy? 'Cause I'm going to be really sad if you come home without it. You don't want to see me sad do you, daddy?"

All King could do was smile, he knew she was playing him, but she was too adorable to resist. "No, I don't want to see you sad. I won't forget, I promise."

"All right," she replied, leaping out of his arms and running back into the living room.

"Don't be in the club fronting like you *that nigga* to them bitches. I'mma find out if you were, and then I'm gonna fuck you up," Kia said, staring at him with a serious face. "I'm just playing, babe, have a good time; and tell Mac and Asia I'm sorry I couldn't make it."

"I'll let them know, don't worry about it."

"And text me when you're on your way back," she said, walking him to the door.

"Nicole, come give daddy a hug and kiss goodbye. He's leaving."

"Dad, me and mommy going to the beach tomorrow; you wanna come with us? It's girls' day out; but you could come if you want to."

"I'll see, babygirl," he plants a big kiss on her cheek and bear hugs her, making her laugh as she tries to get out of it.

Pulling out of the building garage in a cocaine-white, drop-top Ferrari with the heron-colored interior, King puts on track eleven, "HOLD YA HEAD" off of the

Makaveli CD and puts it on repeat. He rocks his head back and forth with the beat feeling like new money. Driving down Vernon Boulevard with the speakers bumping and exhaling the smoke from the Cohiba cigar in the air, King imagines how crazy the party is going to be and hopes no drama will pop off. Making a right on 40th Avenue and driving up the block, he passes Monte's Lounge. A bunch of people are hanging out in front of it and all eyes are on him as King slowly drives by stunting.

"Yo, Life...there goes your boy right there in a fly ass Ferrari," a youngin' said.

"Oh shit, it's lit; that nigga, Haze, wasn't lying," Life said, walking out to the front of the lounge gawking at King and his ride. "Yeah, nigga...it's definitely gonna be a movie tonight."

Monte's Lounge is located on 40th Avenue between 10th and 9th Street in Queensbridge. It's the neighborhood hangout where people from all over Queens come to chill and see and be seen. It's the place were King was arrested for the 4th of July shooting. A picture of the scene that day still hangs on the wall behind the bar. It shows King surrounded by ten police officers with their guns out, pointed at him as he sits in a beach chair in front of the lounge.

After passing the hill, King pulls up to 21st Street where four different colored Ferraris are parked back to back. A crowd of people surround his crew, chopping it up with them and trying to get a glimpse of King and his crew before they head to the party. Everybody is dressed from head to toe in either Versace, Gucci and Louis Vuitton. Iced-out jewelry covers their necks and wrists. The onlookers' mouths are stuck in the open position as they watch King and his crew strut around looking like celebrities; each of the youngins hope when they get older life will be the same for them. The women, of course, don't know how to act; especially when King and Haze are around. Their street cred makes them desirable, but the fact that they both are fine as hell is what keeps the women staring. All eyes gaze upon King as he steps out of his car and approaches the crowd of people staring at him.

"King, let me get fifty dollars," Little Dion asks, emerging from the crowd and running up to him with his hand out.

"Every time I see you, I'm giving you money. What you need fifty dollars for this time?" King replied, staring at the new True Religion outfit and Jordan 11s on Dion.

"I need some new sneakers, my mom don't have the money to buy them."

"Where is your mother at?"

"She's over there talking to Momma G," Dion said, pointing toward the card tables.

"Tanya!" King screams out, waving her to come over to him.

Tanya was King's first love; and he was hers. Her parents sent Tanya to Connecticut to live with her aunt after they found out she and King were messing around with each other. They were both sixteen at the time, and her parents didn't want her making a mistake and getting pregnant by King. After she left, Tanya and King lost contact with each other throughout the years that she was away and they didn't see each other again until a year ago.

A smile appears on King's face as he watches the baddest bitch in the hood walk over to him. Her caramel complexion, long, black straight hair, fat ass and 34 double D breasts make it hard for anyone not to notice her.

"What's good with you?" he asks, giving her a hug.

"Nothing, I just came home from work and I got school in the morning. I'm about to go upstairs and order some Wong's."

"Your bills paid? Your pockets all right?" he asked, looking into her green eyes.

Damn, this nigga still look fine as hell, she said to herself, biting her bottom lip. "It's real hard, but I'm getting by."

"Hann," he looks her straight in the eyes and pulls out two grand from his pants pocket and hands it to her. He already had the money set to the side for her in his left pants pocket, just in case he ran into her.

"King, I can't take this," she said, trying to hand it back to him, all the while knowing he was not going to take it back.

"You better take it," he replied with a serious look on his face. "You doing right with yourself out here and you need help with little man. Save it, or do whatever you want with it; but buy Dion two pairs of sneakers."

"Sneakers? That little nigga has ten pair of sneakers in his closet from the money you already be giving his sneaky ass."

"Word!" King said, laughing and turning around to look back at Dion; he had to respect the lil' nigga's hustle. "He and Nicole are the same age; they gotta hang out together one day. They would have mad fun together," he added thinking how both of them knew how to play him.

"That would be cool, just let me know," she replied, staring at him and thinking what life would have been like if she had never left and the two of them had stayed together. "Well, y'all have a good time and be safe tonight, and tell Dion to bring his ass over here," Tanya said as she turned back in the direction from which she had come from.

"I got you." *Damn, Tanya's still a bad bitch,* he said to himself while walking back to 21st street. He spots Dion sitting in his car, playing with the radio.

"Dion, come here. Your mom is gonna get you the sneakers. Now take this fifty dollars and get Momma G to take you to the drug store and get your mother a card telling her how much you love her and get her some flowers too. You hear me?"

"Yeah, thanks, and good looking out. I will do it tomorrow. I promise," Dion replied.

"Head back over to your mother; it's time to go upstairs," he gives Dion a pound and pats him on the head.

"Yo, let's be out. It's 10:35," King said to his crew; they all hop in their cars and peel off. The train of multi-colored Ferraris looks like a presidential motorcade as they go on to the Queens Borough Bridge.

CHAPTER 2

"Happy birthday and retirement to a New York

Legend."

~King

Cutting through the city blocks in Manhattan and driving down the West Side highway all back to back with King's car in front, the crew can see the neon lights in the sky coming from Club Mansion's building. Club Mansion's has become New York's most premier night club. Located on 20th Street and the West Side Highway in the Chelsea District of Manhattan, celebrities, athletes, music artists and New York's big shots go to this club to party. Taking up half a city block, the lavish looking 60,000 square foot building cost ten million dollars to build and it is worth every penny. The outside and inside of the club has a Miami vibe to it; from the palm trees out front, to the humongous dance floor which includes four small stages for strippers to entertain the crowd and a two hundred and fifty people capacity VIP area overlooking it. It was created by the owner, Miami billionaire Alex Cartegena for his elite clientele of friends.

It's eleven o'clock on the dot, and pulling up to the large front entrance of the club blasting the song, "Beach Chair", is an all-white, drop-top Phantom. Hopping out wearing an all-white linen outfit and matching white loafers – both by Salvatore Ferragamo – with two big platinum chains around his neck and a $100,000 iced-out Rolex on his wrist, is Mac. By his side and grabbing the attention of everybody outside in an all-white Dolce & Gabbana dress is his beautiful wife, Asia. Mac always knew how to make an entrance and club night was no exception.

They both are greeted by the owner, Alex, who walks up to them with a gracious smile on his face. "Happy birthday, my man," Alex said, giving Mac a hug. "You're looking beautiful as always, Asia," he gives her a kiss on the cheek.

"It's gonna be an unforgettable party tonight, Alex," Mac stated.

"Indeed it is; it's packed in there right now and we got everything set up for you just the way you like it in your section. Nothing but the best for you, Mac."

The attention of everyone outside shifted to the five different colored, drop-top Ferraris pulling up to the entrance. Hopping out of the cars are King and his crew, draped in jewelry. One by one, they all congratulate Mac and exchange hugs and pounds with him.

"Let's go have the time of our lives," King said as they all walk in.

Club Mansion's is packed to capacity. The music is pumping and the vibe is off the chart. The main floor and the second level are filled with women wearing their most expensive and tightest outfits. Wait staff makes their rounds through the guests with complementary glasses of champaign on their trays and strippers dance on small stages in the VIP area entertaining Life and the Vernon Posse posted up in there. The 10th Street crew is at the bar ordering bottles along with people from Ravenswood Projects. Mac's friends from all over New York and Miami are in attendance to show him love.

As they make their way through the club, all the attention shifts to Mac and Asia as they walk in with King and his crew. Exchanging hugs and pounds with damn near everybody in the club, they finally get to their section in the VIP area. Waiting for them are eight beautiful Black, Hispanic and White models Mac had flown in from Miami for the weekend to hang with King and his crew. And, of course, there's thirty bottles of Dom Perignon waiting to be popped.

"Damn, who are all these sexy ass women for?" Haze asked, taking a seat in between two of them. The two beautiful Spanish women are instantly attracted to Haze and begin flirting with him the moment he sits down. He's hard to resist; from the smell of his Gucci cologne, right down to the beige dress shirt displaying his muscles; not to mention the scar across the right cheek of his face that most women find attractive.

"They're for y'all," Mac answered with his arm around King's neck. "I told you it's gonna be a movie tonight. Tone gets two of them 'cause we all know he don't get no pussy, so I got him a double dose!" Mac said with a smile on his face.

"Shit, I might take three of them; King don't need one so I'll take his," Tone replied as he sandwiches himself between three of the women and everyone starts laughing.

Fifteen bottles later, the club is popping and everyone is feeling good. DJ Chyna is playing Drake's new single as the dance floor comes alive and everyone sings along; word for word. Mel and Tone are dancing with four of the models as Haze entertains the other models and Asia with stories about his women.

"Mac, happy birthday, you bitch!" Nando said in his Spanish-speaking accent.

Mac turns around and sees the short Mexican man walking up to him in a white suit and a red dress shirt underneath with the top buttons open. "Look at this nigga here. What the fuck...why you show up dressed like Scarface, Nando? Did you lose a bet or something?" Mac laughs. "Just kidding; you know I'm fucking with you... thanks, my man. I appreciate you coming through," Mac said, giving him a hug. "Nando, this is King, my right-hand man and he's also like the little brother I never had" he says as King and Nando shake hands.

Nando Sanchez is the top drug runner in the United States for Hector Santiago, the head of the Rayon Cartel. Nando has been running the dope operation for the Cartel in New York for the past eleven years. He and Mac were cellmates in Attica State prison twelve years ago and became good friends while they were locked up. He's been Mac's dope connect for the past decade and they've made millions upon millions of dollars together.

"This party is crazy, my man. It looks like one of Hector's parties he has back home. The only thing you're missing are some Tigers," Nando said as he takes out three Cuban cigars and passes Mac, and then King, one.

"No party can compare to the parties Hector throws," Mac stated, clipping the tip of the Cuban cigar and lighting it up. "The motherfucker built a club the size of this one on his estate; that's how that motherfucker roll. His estate is four hundred acres, mind you. He built a movie theater, restaurant, zoo, a small soccer stadium, and a bunch of other shit I can't remember right now," Mac told King.

"Damn, that's the life right there. You can't have no shit like that in America though; the FBI and CIA will hang your ass out here for frontin' like that," King replied, popping a bottle of Dom.

Cracking a smile, Mac felt proud watching the young man he's been a mentor to in the streets. King was ready and it was time for Mac to pass over his throne. He puts his arm around King's shoulder and tells him everything is his now. That's why he invited Nando; he wanted the two of them to meet. Mac was handing everything over to King and getting out of the game. He's made enough money to finally move on. Greed can be a downfall for egotistical men, and he wanted to get out while he could. King didn't have to say anything; the look in his eyes as Mac told him his intentions let Mac know he was grateful. They both lifted their bottles and toasted.

"Sexy, let me get four bottles of Perrier Jouet," Flush said to the beautiful Spanish woman bartending. "I'm leaving with her tonight; most definitely," he stated, lighting up a blunt of loud.

"Shorty is bad," Ace said to Enuff. Both men are Mac's shooters, and they are chilling at the bar with Flush.

"What's good, Lil Heat?"

Flush hears the raspy voice as he turns around slowly. It's a nickname Hoffa called him when he was younger because he looked just like his father, Heat.

"When you came home, nigga?" Flush asked Hoffa, giving him a hug.

"Two weeks ago. You know they ain't have enough to keep me locked up on. They had to let me go after sitting up for two years on some minor shit. You know how they do. If they can't get you on what they want to get you on, they'll get you on something else just to save face," Hoffa replied.

Eric Allen, aka Hoffa, is regarded as one of Queens top five street legends of all time. Standing 5'8" and dark skinned with a slim build and a lawless attitude, the thirty-five year old is a grimy stick-up kid and a cold-blooded killa from the 40th side of 12th Street. His rough-looking face and droopy left eye, along with his deep voice just adds to his menacing persona. He puts fear in many just by showing up. There are plenty of families that have lost their loved ones and some that were done some type of harm due to the work Hoffa had been putting in on the streets of New York since the age of seventeen.

Hoffa has been home for two weeks now, after fighting for his freedom for the last two years against the New York Justice system. He was charged with two counts of murder for killing two men on 145th Street and Broadway in Harlem in broad daylight. Several people witnessed the murders, but none would talk. Video footage from a surveillance camera in front of a bodega showed Hoffa in a heated argument with two men, which then escalated into a physical fight. Fifteen minutes later, the two men were shot multiple times around the corner from the bodega and were pronounced dead on the scene. Even though there was no one willing to testify, the murder weapon was never recovered, and there was no actual footage of the shooting, the DA still charged Hoffa with two counts of murder. The DA insisted that because of the video footage of the fight between him and the two men right before the shootings and given his violent history, there was enough circumstantial evidence that he committed the crime to hold it over for trial; they also hoped that eventually someone would come forward who witnessed the murders. Having to sit on Rikers Island in the

George R. Vierno Center (The Beacon), after being denied bail, with no possibility of parole because of his violent rap sheet and a small weapons charge, Hoffa hoped that he would be able to beat the murder wrap and also beat the weapons charge through suppression of evidence. With help from Haze, he was able to hire one of the best criminal attorneys in New York City; Jack Lawson.

For two years while Hoffa sat in jail on the weapons charge with an impending case against him for the murders, his lawyer went through every loophole in the case. He put in one motion after the other delaying the case as long as possible and hoping for a break. Eventually they got the break they were hoping for thanks to Haze. Haze found out through a connection he had in the New York Supreme Court office that a man had come forward stating that he witnessed Hoffa murder the two men and he was going to testify at the trial as a surprise witness for the DA. Haze was able to locate the witness, kidnap him, murder him, and have his body disposed of before the DA could put him into protective custody until the trail started. For two weeks before the trial, the DA was unable to contact or even find their witness after his disappearance, so it forced Judge Hall, who presided over the case, to dismiss the charges due to a lack of evidence and the disappearance of the only witness willing to testify that the DA had.

"You can call me Flush, my nigga. That's what I go by," Flush corrected Hoffa. He always hated the name, Lil' Heat.

"That's your handle now? Flush. That's what's up; my nigga. Where is King and Haze?" Hoffa asked in a dismissive tone as he observed the club.

"They're in the VIP; Mac and the rest of the crew are there with them."

"I'm going to head over there then. I'mma get up with you later," Hoffa said, giving Flush a pound and a hug.

"Like I was telling you a little while ago...Nando will get you whatever you need, even on the arm. He got enough dope to flood all of New York," Mac told King, staring him in straight in the eyes and noticing no emotion. It's the way King always looks when talking business. No emotion; just cool, calm, and collected.

"Oh, shit, look at who the State let back into society, Mac," King said, letting out a slight laugh as he watches Hoffa walk toward them looking like a new man.

Watching as Hoffa approaches dressed in all-black, Mac isn't happy or pleased to see him. He knows how grimy Hoffa is and how they really don't get along because Hoffa was always robbing Mac's workers.

"They finally let him go; the streets ain't safe no more," Mac said in a sarcastic tone as he gets up.

"Nigga is getting money with no worries. I see life is good, Mac," Hoffa said, giving Mac a hug.

"I've been getting money before you started robbing niggas," Mac replied with a smile on his face. "I see you rocking a Caesar with waves now. I guess them CO bitches on the Island weren't trying to braid your hair?"

"You a funny ass nigga, Mac…word up. I had to switch up though. I got tired of wearing braids. I had to get on my grown man shit; no what I mean."

A smile appears on Hoffa's face as he turns to his right and stands face to face with King. "My nigga, King. Your name rings bells on Rikers. Niggas from different boroughs were coming through telling me stories about you in these streets. You're practically a living legend."

"No doubt, fam…it's good to see you home," King replied, giving Hoffa a hug and then telling him to sit down so they could talk.

Surrounded by a group of women as always whenever he's in a partying atmosphere, is Haze. He loves to tell other women about his sexcapades just to see their reaction and get a rise out of them. It was almost like foreplay for him.

"Haze, you a foul, nigga," Asia said to him after he told them stories about his skills with women out in the streets.

"Nah, he's nothing but a dog. I can't fuck with a nigga like you. You're the type that breaks bitch's hearts and you don't even give a fuck," Tamara, Asia's best friend, stated.

Haze, King's right-hand man and second in charge, is more than a business man when it comes to dealing with the money and the product in the streets. He's a smooth-dressing ladies' man of the crew that used to play basketball for St. John's College. He got into the street life after being arrested for selling coke on the campus. He lost his full scholarship and was kicked out of school. Ever since then, he's been learning the game from Hoffa and King who both took a liking to him early on. King liked Haze's style and his business-savvy mind and put him down with his team even though he was from the 40th side of 12th Street and the rest of the crew was from the 41st side of 12th Street.

"Look at ya boy Tone's thirsty ass. He knew I was hollering at that shorty. That's how you know he don't get

47

no pussy! He's always chasing some because he ain't getting any," Mel said to Flush as they leaned against the banister of the VIP section. "He waits to see if another nigga could snatch her up, and then he tries to do his thing. He always does that shit; pathetic ass nigga."

"Fuck it, there's other broads in here; let him do his thing," Flush replied, knowing he wanted to bust out laughing because Mel was telling the truth.

"What y'all niggas over here talking about?" King asked, putting his arms around both of their necks.

"How your boy, Tone, don't get no pussy?" Mel replied.

Shaking his head, also knowing Mel wasn't lying, King responded, "Well, y'all need to be talking about how we about to take over Queens and quit worrying about who's getting laid. Mac just gave me his connect, workers and his clientele. It's time to get that real money we've been waiting for. What we doing now ain't shit and y'all know it; we eating now, but we about to eat real good for real."

"What we eating?" Haze asked, walking up to them, already lit off the Rose Moet.

"Look at this nigga, he's already twisted. We talking about taking over Queens like we always wanted to. Mac just handed everything over to me and I do mean *everything*," King said to him.

"That's all I need to hear. You ain't said nothing but a word and we all riding till the caskets drop," Haze replies and then they all lift their bottles and toast.

Exhaling cigar smoke and standing by himself in a zone observing everything going on, Mac watches as the strobe lights move around the packed dance floor. Hoffa is in a world of his own as he makes it rain on the strippers working the pole. Mac's people from Miami are popping bottles at the bar and entertaining a crowd of women around them. Turning around, Mac sees King, Flush and Mel laughing at Haze who is trying to dance with two women. A smile stretches across Mac's face as he enjoys the fact that the men are having a good time and as he remembers the days he and his ruthless team ran Long Island City, Queens. All the fun they had, the money they made, and all the work they put in on the streets flash before Mac's eyes. He, Heat, Butter, Ghost and Kool made up the crew that called themselves Black Out back in the day. Mac and Heat are the only two members still alive to this day. Heat, Flush's father, is doing life in Sing Sing Correctional Facility for killing the three hit men that killed Butter and Ghost at a block party in Hempstead, Long

Island. Kool died in a car crash on the Grand Central Parkway due to a drunk driver side swiping his car and sending him crashing into the steel divider and flipping over to the other side of the highway. Mac got a little emotional thinking about how what was once a tight crew ended up torn apart by one reason or another.

"Baby, are you all right?" Asia asks as she hugs Mac and starts moving her body slowly in front of him; teasing him as he puts his hands on her waist and brings her closer to him. He can smell the Versace perfume on her as he admires her seductive eyes.

"Everything is all right. I was just enjoying the moment, watching everybody having a good time dancing and drinking; no drama; everybody is just having a good time and I like that."

"Are you ready to knock me up and have some kids now that you're retiring?" Asia asked with excitement in her voice and eyes, admiring her husband's dark-skin face and round eyes.

"Yeah, I'm ready; we're not getting any younger and we're gonna be bored by ourselves in the Bahamas. We need some kids to run around that big ass house we got," he replied.

*****

This shit is crazy, King said to himself, taking a sip from his bottle of Dom and looking around the club. All of a sudden, Big's, "One More Chance" comes on and the club goes crazy. More people flood the dance floor; people in the VIP area jump on the couches and tables with bottles in their hands and everybody recites the song word for word throughout the club.

Mac puts his arm around King as they both stand at the banister of the VIP area staring at everybody in the club having a good time. "Sky's the limit fam; don't fuck up what I'm handing you. You got a good crew behind you. Don't let anything come between y'all. Never get too greedy; make sure everybody eats the way y'all do now. Remember…reputation is the cornerstone of power. So much depends on reputation; guard it with your life at all costs and always plan to the end," Mac told him.

"I will, fam; I will," King replies as he pauses and exhales the cigar smoke. "Not only is it your birthday, it's your going away party also," King said with a big smile on his face while giving him a hug. He was happy that Mac made millions and was going to leave the game on his own terms.

"Queens and New York are in good hands," Haze stated, walking up to King and putting his arm around Mac. "Yo!" Haze screams out, waving Flush, Tone, Mel and Asia and the other women over. "Let's have a toast for Mac's fortieth birthday and his retirement," he said as Enuff and Ace join in and everyone lifts their bottles and glasses.

"Happy birthday and retirement to a Queensbridge and New York City Legend. You're always going to be remembered and your name will forever live in infamy, my nigga," King said as everyone bangs bottles and glasses.

"Come on baby, let's dance; this is our song," Asia said to Mac as Frankie Beverly and Mays' song, "Before I Let Go" blasts through the speakers.

For some reason, King felt something was wrong. His instincts kicked in; a sixth sense some would call it. Everything became silent and started to move in slow motion around him. Staring at the faces of everybody moving around him, his instincts make King reach toward his waist for his gun, but before he can get it out, out of nowhere...

BOOM!

The sound of a 40 cal. Sig Sauer rings off and Mac's brains fly all over Asia's face as his body drops to the floor. People start running and screaming as time seems frozen for those that saw what happened – Mac, the boss…leaving the game; but not the way he planned. Asia rubs her hand across her face feeling Mac's brain matter on her cheeks and she screams a gut-wrenching scream. King drops his bottle and quicker than the speed of light, he pulls out his Glock 9mm and puts a hollow tip bullet through the head of a Spanish dude who is wearing the club's security outfit and who had just killed Mac.

Pandemonium erupts as people are screaming and running in different directions trying to get out of the club. Strippers grab their clothes and their money off the floor as they follow the rest of the patrons out of the club. Five more shots are fired at King and his crew; they come from somewhere on the dance floor. Haze and Mel grab Asia and Mac's body and pull them to the back of the VIP area, while Flush jumps on the couch and fires eight shots at the two dudes near the stage who are coming toward him firing continuous shots.

Rat tat tat tat tat tat tat!

Bullets from a Mac-10 tear up Enuff and Ace – Mac's bodyguards – as their bodies fall over the railing of the VIP area and onto the dance floor.

"Tone, get a gun from Mel," King said to him as he sends three shots at one of the hit men; hitting him in the both legs and the stomach. The man doubles over falling to the floor and screaming in pain.

"Come on y'all," Alex, the club owner, screams out to Haze and Mel who are guarding Asia and Mac. He holds the side door of the VIP area open. "Let's go, let's go. The cars are ready," Alex said as Mel carries Mac's body out the door and Haze and Asia run behind him to the Suburban in the alley.

"Tone…to your left!" King screamed out.

Without any hesitation, Tone spins his three hundred-pound body around and drops to one knee. He fires three shots at another hit man who takes cover behind a wall and returns fire. The club which was filled with people only minutes before, now looks like a war scene.

"We gotta get out of here; the police are gonna be here any second," Flush said to King and Tone as he covers them with his eyes, scanning what's in front of them. They all make their way to the side door Alex is still holding open. They make it out the side door and hop into another Suburban as the police rush through the front door of the club. King tells the driver how to get to Roses coffee shop and the driver quickly speeds off. As they drive down the back entrance onto 11th Avenue, King hears the overwhelming sound of police sirens, screaming and gunshots coming from the West Side Highway in front of the club. Staring through the rearview mirror and noticing no cop cars chasing them, King lets out a sigh of relief and does a Hail Mary, crossing his heart and thanking God to be alive.

CHAPTER 3

"Then I'mma pick your family apart; one by one."

~Haze

Good morning, New York. I'm Erica Scott. And I'm John Blake, and this is Channel 5 morning news. Thank you for joining us this beautiful, Friday morning where it is 80 degrees at 6:00 a.m. We start off the day with our lead story which is the violence that erupted a few hours ago at Club Mansion's on 20th Street and the West Side Highway in the Chelsea District. Five people were murdered, five others were wounded, and eight people were arrested. Reporting live from the scene is Dan Harper as we head out to him now.

"Who the fuck did this?" King asked, rubbing his forehead before throwing back a shot of Hennessy as he watches the news coverage on the 70-inch flat screen TV inside Roses coffee shop. King opened the coffee shop seven months ago. It's the crew's social club/hangout, located on 48th Avenue and Vernon Boulevard in Long Island City, Queens.

"I don't know, fam...Mac had a lot of enemies. Those dudes were wearing the club's security uniforms and they were trying to kill you also. They were barely shooting at the rest of us; this shit seems personal," Flush replied, standing behind the Oakwood counter, making a pot of coffee.

"Motherfuckers killed Mac, fam; that shit doesn't make any sense at all," Tone said, wiping a tear from his eye and staring at the scene of the club on TV.

"That nigga was out, he was done with the streets; why kill him?" King stated, staring at a picture of him and Mac hanging on the wall behind the cash register. They were on a boat in Florida, holding up an enormous-sized red snapper. *But, the streets weren't done with him,* he said to himself, taking a seat. It's a phrase that Mac would always say.

"You think Gotti did this?" Tone asked, taking a seat at the table with King. "Remember Mac had Gotti popped last summer in front of Monte's Lounge for talking shit, maybe this was payback for that."

"Nah, I spoke to Gotti about that. He's about getting his paper right now and he knew he was too drunk and in the wrong the night that shit happened. We all know he runs his mouth too much; but he wouldn't make a move like that, especially against Mac," King replied, lighting a cigar and watching as Haze and Mel approach the coffee shop.

"What the fuck!" Haze said as he and Mel walked through the door. "We took care of everything at the hospital. Asia's parents and friends are there holding her down right now. The cops came through asking questions and they're pissed off 'cause nobody's talking. So, shit is gonna be crazy hot out here for us for a while behind this," he said, taking off his shirt that is covered with Mac's blood.

"A motherfucker with balls the size of King Kong did this shit. A smart nigga with money and pull, 'cause them dudes were up in the VIP area acting like security all night. It had to be like five of them," Mel stated.

"Hoffa maybe?" he just came home and he and Mac really didn't like each other," Flush asked, taking a seat.

"Nah, I doubt it; but you never know. The thing about Hoffa is, all he would have wanted was his blocks back. Mac would have given him those out of respect and Hoffa knows that. So it would be stupid for him to take out Mac and then me; I just can't see him doing this shit," King answered.

"Well, all I know is Gotti wasn't there and he's the only nigga we know for certain that had a beef with Mac. No matter if he let it go or not, he's still a grimy ass nigga with a lot of soldiers ready to march on command;

we all know that. I wouldn't put it past him," Haze stated, shaking his head.

"Shit!" King said out load, slamming his fist on the table and standing up. He knows he has to make a move on Gotti; everybody else feels the same way even though there's no proof that Gotti was involved. Memories of him and Gotti growing up together playback in King's mind like a film. He relives the two of them playing on Mac's basketball team together, sleeping over each other's house, trading clothes and sneakers, and coming up in the streets together. A chill shoots through his body as he stares out the window at two kids playing basketball against each other across the street.

"It is what it is. We gotta move on that nigga," Tone said, rubbing his enormously rough hands together and staring King in the eyes.

"I know, fam; I already have a plan in mind," King said, looking each of the men directly in the eye and seeing that they're all in agreement with what needs to be done.

*****

Getting out of her bed and not hearing her father's voice, Nicole starts to think that her father didn't come home with her ice cream. Walking out of her room, she sees no sign of him in the living room and heads to his bedroom. Cracking the bedroom door open, she sees her mother sitting on the bed with her back turned to her and her head down.

"Mommy, why are you crying?" she asked as Kia snaps out of the zone she was in. Her mind has been in a world of its own reminiscing about Mac and the good times she had with him and Asia. She was also trying to figure out how she was gonna tell Nicole that Uncle Mac had passed away.

"I'm not crying, baby; it's my allergies," Kia lied, turning around.

"Well, where's daddy with the breakfast and ice cream?" Nicole asked with a serious look on her face that resembled the one her father often had.

"It's here; he brought it home a little while ago. He had to go back to work," Kia replied, getting up from the bed, knowing she had it delivered from the diner a little while ago because of what happened last night.

"Good, 'cause I thought I was gonna have to call him and start begging. He knows how serious I am when it comes to my ice cream," Nicole said, standing with her arms crossed.

"Girl, go wash your face and brush your teeth; talking all crazy," Kia said, walking her out the room.

"We're still going to the beach, right? You promised."

"Yes, we're still going. Just you and I...girls' day out and after that, we will go to Bruno's for some pizza," Kia said as they walked into the bathroom.

"Nice," Nicole replied with a big smile on her face.

*****

"I need you to go meet up with my cousin and let him know what the situation is. There's gonna be a block party Saturday in Ravenswood. Shit...that's tomorrow. Tell him go out there with some shooters and pop them niggas, Kev and Biz. We're gonna make Gotti suffer before he gets it himself," King said, looking Flush dead in the eyes. "Now listen to me closely. Tell him to lay Biz down and hit Kev lightly; but if they both go..." he smacks his hands together, "...it is what it is. He knows what they both look like."

"I got you. I'mma hit him right now," Flush replied.

"Haze, you need to get with Life and everybody else in the hood that used to work for Mac and let them

61

know shit done changed; and they working for us now. I'll handle all his workers outside the hood," King instructs Haze on what to do.

"No problem. You want me to holla at Fatal also and let him know what we talked about," Haze asked.

"Yeah, I forgot about that. Let him know he better not fuck this up. We could've picked someone else, but we chose him," King said, getting up from the table and grabbing his car keys. "I'mma head to the crib for a little while; y'all can chill here if you want to," he said, giving everybody pounds before starting to walk toward the door.

"Yeah, we gonna hang around. I'll set the alarm and lock up," Haze replied, walking King to the door.

*****

FBI Headquarters
26 Federal Plaza - 7th floor
Manhattan, New York

"Mac, Enuff, and Ace; all killed by the guns we found on West and Matty from what we can tell so far. Now Dante Tolbert, aka West and Matthew Ruiz, aka Matty are part of a murder-for-hire crew called 187 from

Brooklyn. Without a doubt, they were hired to kill Mac; so we gotta find out by whom. Now they were killed by King's crew from what a few witnesses said; but the club's cameras didn't work for some reason, and we didn't recover any of their weapons," FBI Agent Sam Bauer said to his partner, John Mackey, and a few other agents inside the conference room in the FBI office at 26 Federal Plaza in Manhattan.

"Donaldson, I want you to call Mike at the 114th precinct and tell him to have some of his officers run down on King and his crew. Hopefully they can catch them holding before we start bringing them in and talking to them," Agent Bauer told him.

Sam Bauer is one of the toughest and most relentless FBI agents you will ever come across. Standing 5'8" with a headful of blond hair and blue eyes, the forty-four-year-old Irish agent is a twenty-year veteran. He has one objective in life, and that's putting criminals away for a long time. His case profile and conviction rate are impeccable; the highest in the agency and the envy of other agents. He lives by the book; and only by the book, and most times it pays off by him getting his man.

"Well, since Mac is gone now and the case we were building against him is dead, King is gonna take his place in the streets, without a doubt; you can bet on that," Agent Mackey said, staring at King's picture on the bulletin board in the front of the room. The board had the faces of the street hustlers with lines from their photos to show how they are all connected; Mac's picture is at the top with King's directly under it.

"How about Hoffa? He just got out of the joint; he could've had Mac killed. He has a lot of connections and he's well-respected, he could have easily pulled this off if he wanted to," Agent Crebbs asked Agent Bauer.

"He doesn't have a motive to pull this off. That's not his style; he's not trying to be a kingpin. Nawh, it's King, I know it is…he has it written all over him and he has a team to back him. These thugs are just like crabs in a barrel; always crawling on top of one another to make their way to the top," Agent Bauer stares at the forty-eight by ninety-six bulletin board in front of him moving the photos around in his head playing a game of connect the dots to murder. "So we have a new target now, gentlemen and he's as treacherous and elusive as they come. Mr. Aaron "King" Johnson just moved up to public enemy number one," Agent Bauer replied as he replaces Mac's photo at the top of the board with King's.

*****

After having a fun day at the beach with Nicole, Kia met up with King and headed over to Asia's house in Westchester where Kia and Asia's parents had started making the arrangements for Mac's wake and the funeral. Seeing the stress on Asia's face only saddened King and Kia even more knowing how strong the bond was between her and Mac and how they couldn't live without each other. Asia and Mac had been together for nineteen years and were a month away from their two-year wedding anniversary.

"What's good, fam?" Haze asked, answering his phone as King was on the other end.

"You were able to take care of that for me with no problems; right?"

"Yeah, it's taken care of. Flush is in motion right now; so that will be covered also," Haze replied, getting in his gray S-Class Benz along with two of the models from Mac's party last night. The two men never talked in specifics when they were on the phone...only in codes. They knew of too many hustlers that were busted based on wire taps.

"Good, Kia is handling the funeral arrangements with Asia's parents. So I'll let everyone know what the deal is when I get the word."

"All right...I'm heading to the crib right now. Call me on that phone if anything happens," Haze replied.

Meanwhile, on 92nd Street and Columbus Avenue on the west side of Manhattan, one of King's black Hummers is parked on the corner while Flush talks to S, King's younger cousin.

David Johnson, aka S, is the leader of a crew called The Hit Squad; a murderous crew of hit men and stick-up kids known for laying niggas down and robbing anybody shining or moving weight in Harlem. S and his crew control every drug from dope, coke, weed and molly being sold on Columbus Avenue from 80th Street to 105th Street. The twenty-four-year-old, half-Black and half-Puerto Rican was born and raised in Harlem by his mother. He's King's cousin on his father's side. King taught his younger cousin everything he needed to know about the streets; from showing him how to bust a gun, to hustling drugs and how to outsmart his enemies and the law. His physical appearance easily intimidates people; standing 6'4" and a husky two hundred and seventy pounds. S, which is short for Satan, was a name his mother called him. She kicked him out of her house when he was sixteen; after she saw him kill two men he had a beef with at a block party in front of the whole neighborhood. His mother could not believe her eyes when she saw her son kill those men just as easily as eating a meal. She still does not speak to her son to this day because of the shame and embarrassment she feels behind what he did. For the past eight years, he's made a name for himself and earned the reputation of a grimy stick-up kid and a stone-cold killa on the streets of Harlem and the Bronx.

"Them niggas be stashing the burner; so they not gonna have that on them while they're out there tomorrow. The thing is, King wants you to lay Biz down and hit Kev lightly – in the leg or whatever; but make sure you rob them or attempt to first before anything," Flush told S.

"I got you," S replied, staring through his smoke-gray lenses at Flush with a smile on his face. He knew King was gonna have no less than forty racks for him for doing the job and for him, money talks and all other bullshit walks. "What about that nigga, Gotti? What if he somehow gets in the way? What's the plan for him?"

"It is what it is then; lay him down too if need be. But I'm pretty sure he won't be a problem for y'all. It's on the D.S. block tomorrow. They gonna be out there all night, so be out there like eleven o'clock at night so you can get the jump on them," Flush said, hopping in the black Hummer.

"No doubt, we'll be there. You know my nigga, Cream, got a show at BB King's tonight; it's gonna be lit in there. Everything is free and I got a group of bitches coming through. You can roll with us if you want," S said.

"Nah, fam. I got some shit I got to handle later on. Good looking out though, I know son gonna tear it down. Just don't get into no shit tonight; we need you tomorrow," Flush replied, giving S a pound and then pulling off.

Lying on his king-sized Hermes bed with Nicole while she's watching *Man On Fire,* King stares out the bedroom window with a million thoughts running through his mind. He thinks about where he's gonna get stash houses for the work; if everything goes right with his cousin tomorrow in Ravenswood, and when Homicide was gonna come get him for questioning about last night.

"Dad, are you sleeping? Why aren't you watching the movie?" Nicole asked, dropping popcorn crumbs on the bed.

"I'm not asleep. I see Denzel teaching the girl how to swim faster," King said, knowing he's not watching the movie because he's saw it over twenty times and knows every scene just by hearing it.

"Oh, okay," Nicole said, turning back around.

Closing his eyes, King starts to think about the 6 months that he and Gotti spent together on Rikers Island and the countless number of fights they got into protecting each other from the Brooklyn dudes that ran the dorm. Coming up in the game with King through the years, Gotti has become just like him; a ruthless, manipulative, militant-minded killa. He was always thinking and scheming; creating situations that benefit him and capitalizing off of it.

Haze hops out of his gray S-Class Benz on 21st Street on a hot, Saturday afternoon wearing a gray Nike tracksuit and the gray Jordan 7s. He makes his way through the 41st side of 12th Street. Walking past people sitting on the bench and staring into the packed block, he can hear them whispering and looking at him through the corner of their eyes. Passing the basketball court, he sees one of the crew's young workers – Fatal – leaning up against the gate. Nineteen-year-old Calvin James, aka Fatal, runs the 41st side of 12th Street for King and his crew. He's a young up-and-comer with heart, street smarts and a low-key demeanor.

"What's good, homie?" Fatal asks Haze; giving him a hug and pound.

"Same shit, different day. How are things looking out here? Everything good?" Haze asks, leaning on the black gate next to him and staring at the kids playing on the block.

"Shit is slow and them boys been out all morning over what happened last night."

"Yeah...niggas violated, but we laid them down. We don't know who's behind it yet, but we'll find out. Anyway, King wanted me to holla at you about running the weed operation for us, along with everything else you are doing now. He wanted to give you a shot since you've been doing your thing out here for us."

"Definitely," Fatal said, staring Haze in the eyes. "I got y'all, without a doubt."

"Good, Flush will get with you later to go over everything and get you set up."

"No doubt, fam. Tell King good looking out, too. I appreciate it."

"Of course," Haze said, looking to the left of him. "Is that my nigga right there? What's popping?" Haze asked Hoffa, giving a hug and a pound.

"Same shit. I heard what happened at the party after I left. I wish I would've stayed, my nigga; that shit is fucked up. Mac was a good dude. He ain't deserve to go out like that; especially on his birthday," Hoffa replied.

"Yo, that's Solo's chain you wearing, fam?" Fatal asked Hoffa, giving him a pound, referring to the gold Cuban link chain around his neck with an iced-out King Tut medallion that belonged to a rapper from Harlem named Solo.

Since the age of fifteen, Hoffa has been sticking people up. He loves the rush he gets from it, so it never gets old to him. From drug dealers to drug connects, rappers and anyone shining…he's robbed well over a hundred people since he started doing it twenty years ago.

"Yeah, I caught that nigga last night at Sin's. He was trying to stunt on me in front of some strippers, so I backed him and his whole team down in the VIP area and took his shines," Hoffa replied proudly.

"Nigga, you crazy as shit! That's Butch Reed's nephew," Haze said, shaking his head. "The nigga runs half of uptown and he got the police in his pocket. You better watch your back."

"Fuck that nigga; he's a rat. I was up North with niggas that fucked with him. They told me he be setting his own niggas up to get knocked and that's a fact. His back is already in the wind; I ain't got shit to worry about."

"I ain't know all that," Haze replied.

"Yeah, a lot of niggas don't know that. His time is coming, so I ain't worried about that nigga. Anyway, y'all niggas going to the block party in Ravenswood tonight?"

"Nah, niggas is chilling," Haze replied, lighting a cigarette and then putting his hand on Hoffa's shoulder. "What's good with the shit you got going on in Albany?"

"I got it popping for real," Hoffa replied, whipping off his Hennessey-colored Versace glasses. "I'm moving two bricks a week. Wholesale though; I ain't trying to deal with the hand-to-hand shit and having to worry about workers."

"What you paying?"

"Thirty a gram; selling it for fifty. So a nigga doing all right for himself."

"Yeah, no doubt. King could probably get you a better price though. I'll holla at him and see what's good. Niggas could get money together," Haze said, staring at Hoffa's droopy left eye.

"Y'all about to run all of Queens, so I know y'all gonna look out for a nigga," Hoffa replied with a big grin his face.

Hoffa and Haze were both born and raised on the 40th side of 12th Street. Before King put Haze down with his crew, he was one of Hoffa's youngins; hustling for him and helping him stick niggas up. Hoffa was like an older brother and a mentor to Haze. The five-inch cut Haze got across the right cheek of his face was from a fight that he and Hoffa got into with five dudes from Corona, Queens at Monte's Lounge.

"Shit, here they come," Fatal said as two unmarked cars came from each entrance of 21st Street into the block toward Haze, Fatal and Hoffa.

Hopping out of the unmarked cars are four of the dirtiest undercover cops in all of Queens. They are known as the gun squad led by twenty-year-veteran, Captain Ruiz; a short and chubby middle-aged Spanish man.

"What's going on, playboy? I heard ya boy, King, is the King of Queens now. Hands on the gate, y'all know the fucking drill. Y'all packing?" Captain Ruiz asked as his officers searched Haze, Fatal and Hoffa.

"Nah, you caught me at the wrong time," Haze replied with a smirk on his face.

"Smart ass…we know what happened the other night. You and your crew were slipping and ya'll fucked up. You left the club right, so that tells me that you weren't shooting. That's why you and Mel left," Detective Bristol said, looking at the stone-cold look on Haze's face. "King is the gangsta that bust his gun; not you," he said, trying to get Haze mad. The detective was trying to get a rise out of Haze and see if he would slip up and say something, or if the expression on his face would change.

"Tell your boy, King, he won't be filling Mac's shoes any time soon," Captain Ruiz stated before blowing cigarette smoke in Haze's face.

"Fuck that, are you arresting me, pig!" Haze asked.

"Pig?"

"Yeah, pig! I don't give a fuck that your skin is black like mine; you're still a pig!" Haze said to Detective Bristol.

Detective Bristol grabbed the collar of Haze's tracksuit jacket and pulled him closer to him. "I'll break your motherfuckin' face you little pussy, and then I'll lock your ass up for assaulting an officer with a deadly weapon; keep trying me!" Detective Bristol said to Haze, standing face to face with him.

"Go right ahead, that's a lawsuit; more money in my pocket. And after I'm through screwing you in the courts, then I'mma pick your family apart, one by one."

"Are you threatening me, you two-bit thug?" Detective Bristol asked as Captain Ruiz steps in between the two of them and the other detectives pull Detective Bristol away.

"Tell King and the rest of your crew y'all are all done out here. Ain't no money gonna be made out here by any of you or in any part of Queens unless King talks directly to me. You hear me, Scarface? Oh, shit...Hoffa, I didn't recognize you. You got tired of looking like a bitch with them braids; huh?" Captain Ruiz said, laughing and then walking away.

"Go fuck yourself, Ruiz," Hoffa replied.

10, 20, 30, 40, 50, 60, 70. Seventy racks; this is for Mac's funeral and then this seventy racks is for Enuff and Ace's families. Damn, this leaves me with a $125,000 in this stash. My shit is getting low, King said to himself, locking up his safe which was stashed under a floorboard in his closet. *Where in the hell did Nicole put my phone?* King thought to himself as he walks through the hallway and into the living room. He sees his babygirl sitting on the couch playing with his phone.

"What are you doing with my phone? Didn't I tell you not to play with that?" he asked her in a stern tone.

"I was texting Uncle Tone," she replied with a disappointed look on her face.

"You were texting Tone? Why? Let me see," he takes the phone.

It's Nicole, can you bring me a bacon pizza pie and boneless chicken bites from Dominos? I will pay for it. Thank you.

"Girl, you bugging. Why are you begging your uncle for pizza? Your mom is cooking your favorite, baked Ziti."

"Yeah, I know mommy is cooking my favorite, but I want some pizza too. I just saw a Dominos' commercial and it looked really good. Dominos makes the best boneless chicken bites; besides, you know you want some too," she replied with the cutest grin on her face, trying to win her father over.

"I'll buy you some tomorrow 'cause tonight we're eating Ziti. So go in the kitchen and see if your mother needs help," he said with a serious look on his face as he rubbed the top of her head.

*****

The liquor store clerk has a big smile on his face as he rings up everything Gotti has purchased. "So that's ten bottles of Patron at $100 each, ten half gallons of Hennessey, and fifteen cases of Moet Rose. That will be an even $7,000. I gave you a little bit of a discount for being such a loyal customer," he said as his eyes were fixated on the enormous stack of hundred-dollar bills in Gotti's hand.

"Put some in that car too, split it up," Gotti said to the store worker who wheeled the cases Moet Rose out to the parking lot.

"Yo, Biz...call Dina and tell her to meet us on the block in twenty minutes with some youngins to help us with this shit," Gotti ordered his crew member to do as he walked alongside of the store worker, hopping into his gray Cadillac Escalade.

Jarred Baker, aka Gotti, is an elusive and treacherous gangsta from Ravenswood Housing Projects. Besides standing 6'2" and having a muscular, two hundred and thirty pound build, it's his pointed nose and narrow eyes which give him a mischievous look adding to his already sinister persona. He's the center of attention wherever he goes because of his loud and boisterous attitude. The twenty-seven year old runs Ravenswood Housing Projects, which are a few blocks up 21st Street from Queensbridge houses. No drugs get sold in Ravenswood unless they come from him. Gotti has been running Ravenswood for seven years and has made a lot of money selling coke and weed on the four blocks out there. He and King grew up together playing on the same basketball teams and going to the same elementary school. Coming up in the streets together, they became good friends and ended up doing their first bid together as adolescents on Rikers Island in C-74. Ever since then, Gotti has made a name for himself and is becoming a legend on the streets of Queens.

Pulling up to the block and seeing Dina and a few youngins waiting to help him carry the liquor on to the block, Gotti notices how packed the inside of the joint is already and he cracks a big smile.

"How much I gotta give you for the food?" Gotti asked Dina as he hops out his truck.

"It came out to a $2,500 dollars. I got two hundred steaks, a thousand chicken wings, a thousand hot dogs, a thousand hamburgers, and a bunch of other shit."

"You think that's gonna be enough food? It's four o'clock and it's already packed out here; that might not be enough once the rest of them nigga's get here," he stated, watching the smile on her face turn to a frown.

"Shit, I guess I can go to Associated and get some more food," she replies.

"Hann, that's the $2,500 you spent on the food and here's another $1,000 to get some more; when we finish taking all the liquor out, take the truck and get some more food."

"Aight, Kev is upstairs waiting for you," Dina replied, getting in the driver's seat.

CHAPTER 4

"I had to my nigga, just for him fronting like that."

~*Gotti*

King sits back on his couch watching the Yankees play the Redsox. After eating a plate of Ziti, he can't help but think about Mac and how they used to go to Yankee Stadium and watch the games together; sitting behind the visiting team's dugout along the third baseline. They were regulars at the games; they would drink Hennessey, talk and enjoy watching a baseball game on many beautiful summer days or nights.

"You suck! How do you end a game by striking out with the bases loaded?" Nicole said, screaming at the TV.

"Yeah, we have to get rid of him, baby girl; you hit better than he does," King said, getting up and walking to the bedroom.

"Kia, have you talked to Asia?" he asked, laying on the bed next to her while she was on her laptop scrolling through websites looking for flowers and other things needed for Mac's funeral.

"Yeah, I spoke to her earlier to see if she needed anything; which reminds me...I have to finish editing this video montage Asia gave me for the wake."

"How are the arrangements coming along?"

"Everything is almost taken care of; I'm just looking for a few extra things. I got the funeral home and the cemetery booked. I paid for the casket this morning that you wanted and the Rolls Royce dealer called me back. They're giving us the hearse, two limos and three cars; all of them black."

"Cool. If you need extra money to pay for anything related to the funeral, there's some in my watch drawer," King said, walking into the bathroom and turning on the shower.

*****

S and three of his soldiers – all dressed in dark blue clothing and Yankee hats – drive down 21st Street and enter the Ravenswood Projects. They could hear the loud music and smell the BBQ from 21st Street as they make a left on 34th Avenue and drive down the block.

"Goddamn. There's gotta be like a thousand people out here," S said, staring into the overcrowded block. "Mayo, double park next to that Infinity right there. If you don't see us coming back this way, that means we had to go to the other side of the block," S instructs him as he and his two other soldiers, Macho and Horse, step out of the truck.

The loud sound of Jay-Z's music blasts through the speakers as BBQ smoke fills the air and people from Ravenswood, New York and out of town, flood the D.S. block. Garbage cans filled with ice and all kinds of liquor bottles are spread throughout the block. Six large barrel grills lined up against the gate give off the smell of different foods cooking inside them. A wooden dance floor that can fit two hundred people was built and placed in the middle of the block. As you come through the entrance of the block, kids could be seen running around playing, and mothers were sitting on benches keeping an eye on them and eating and talking to one another. As he looks to his left, S observes an enormous crowd of people at the card tables.

"We can post up right here," S said as they leaned up against a black gate. It had a clear view of the card tables were Gotti, his crew, and a bunch of women are hanging out. "That's Biz right there in the gray Hermes t-shirt; and that's Kev in the white Velour suit; and that's Gotti that they are standing next to," S told Horse and Macho as he lit a cigarette.

Dressed from head to toe in beige Gucci clothing, sneakers and an iced-out chain that can be seen from a block away, Gotti entertains a crowd of people at the card tables. He is the center of attention; as always. Even though he has a reputation for being a grimy individual; people love being around him.

"Ahhh, here y'all niggas go. Why y'all ain't stay over there where you were? Once I saw you and Hoffa come this way with smiles on your faces, I knew you were about to start talking some dumb shit," Gotti said to King.

"Chill out, we were just laughing about the time we were at that show in D.C. That girl over there that we were talking to said she was at the show," King replied with a slick smile on his face; he knew that someone would ask him to tell the story.

"I heard about that shit, you gotta tell the story," one of Gotti's youngins said.

"Here we go," Gotti said throwing his head back. "Just tell the story the right way this time. Every time you tell it, you make me out to be the foul, nigga," Gotti said, popping a bottle of Rose Moet.

"Yo, who's that in the white bucket hat with the big ass Cuban link chain on?" Macho asked S.

A smile appears on S's face as he looks at his cousin, King. S innocently watches as King tells a story to a crowd of people. He knew the only reason King was there was to create the illusion to everyone including Gotti; that he had nothing to do with what's about to go down.

"That's my cousin, King," S replied to Macho.

Why the fuck would he be out here, Macho said to himself, looking confused and suddenly realizing why King was there.

Over a hundred people are crowded around the card tables to hear King tell the story about the show they were at in D.C. last year. King is known for being able to make you visualize a story so vividly that you feel as if you were right in the middle of the action when it was happening.

"So, we backstage at the show and it's popping. All the artists, their crews and mad model bitches are backstage with us. The shit was like being in a club. We chilling in our little section popping bottles and smoking cigars; it was me, Gotti, Haze, Mel and Flush. We were all shinning, so the bitches and everybody else were watching us hard. We were Loui V'd out, iced-out and Cream had just finished performing, so we knew it was about to be lit," King puts down his cup of Hennessey and lights up a God Of Fire cigar.

All eyes and smiles are on him, eager for him to continue telling the story. "So we just chilling; talking to some bad bitches and one of the girls Gotti was hollering at fucks with one of the corny ass rappers that had just performed. Damn, I forgot his name. Anyway, shorty was the baddest bitch in there."

Gotti nods his head in agreement with King, making the crowd laugh.

"So her man comes backstage with a couple of his goons; some Johnny Gill looking diesel motherfuckers," King adds and the crowd erupts in laughter.

"Her man starts fronting; pacing around, moving his hands and talking about niggas is disrespecting him. He goes on and on about how he runs the city and ain't no out-of-town niggas gonna come up in there and take his girl in front of his face. So I tell Haze and Mel to hold Cream down and get him to the whip in the alley 'cause these corny niggas got hammers on them and they might stunt. So now everybody else that's backstage starts getting shook, walking away knowing something might go down. All of a sudden, this nigga told his man to rob us," King pauses to be dramatic before continuing.

"So what happens?" King asked, looking around at all the faces in the crowd and taking a long pull from his cigar before answering his own question. "Them niggas was slow on the draw and Gotti puts his gun to the head of the bitch he was talking to, and me and Flush got our guns pointed at all four of his men."

The crowd erupts in laughter, looking at Gotti's facial expression while King is looking at him holding back from laughing his damn self.

"So this bitch nigga start saying, 'Please don't kill my girl; please, my nigga. She's my baby's mom, my nigga.' So Flush is like, fuck these niggas. I'm taking their shit and he starts taking their guns, chains, watches and digging in their pockets for their money. So, I tell those niggas to lay face down on the floor as we start walking toward the back door. And this nigga here..." King said, putting his arm around Gotti's shoulder, "Is a foul nigga. He pops the nigga in the ass while he's lying on the ground."

"I had to, my nigga; just for him fronting like that," Gotti said with a smile on his face, making the crowd laugh.

"Now we get to the whips in the alley where Haze, Mel and Cream were waiting for us, and this nigga, Gotti, brings the bitch with him. I'm like, 'What the fuck you kidnapping this bitch now?' And she was like nah, I'm fucking with y'all 'cause them niggas are pussies!'"

Everyone in the crowd laughs and shakes their heads.

"Now we start to drive out the alley and there are a couple of dudes standing in front of the alleyway with their guns out, trying to stop us from leaving. These niggas must think the two Hummers we in ain't bulletproof. So I tell Haze to run the niggas over...fuck that! He runs two niggas over, Gotti opens his window and head shots one of the other dudes."

As everyone is laughing and stuck in amazement listening to King tell the story, Biz walks off in the direction of S and his niggas, to answer his phone.

"I'mma get him to come over here, so be ready," S said to Macho and Horse as he starts to walk toward Biz. As Biz finishes talking on the phone, S approaches him, hand out with a smile on his face. "Biz, what's good, homie? I ain't seen you in a minute, my nigga. Everything good with you?"

Who the fuck is this nigga? Biz said to himself, looking at a tall and husky Spanish man approach him with his hand out, wearing rose-colored lenses.

"It's me, Lex; you used to mess with my sister, Lisa," S said to him. Lisa is a Puerto Rican broad from Uptown that Biz fucked a couple of times and so did Flush. Flush told S all the information he needed to know about her so he could act like he was her brother to game Biz.

"Lisa from 140th and 8th?" Biz asked.

"Yeah, I met you one time at La Marina when she brought you through there for the 4th of July a couple years ago," S replied.

"Oh, shit, nigga…what the fuck you been eating? You were skinny as hell when I met you that time."

"A nigga got his weight up, B. What's good though? I see you and your crew got shit popping out here."

"Yeah. This is something light, not too major. Y'all want a couple of bottles and some food? I see you and boys just posted up over here chilling," Biz replied, looking at Macho and Horse leaning against the gate.

"Nah, we were looking for some loud and some sniff. We were just drinking at this bitch's house over there across the street. She had a couple of friends over, but they weren't popping off so we bounced."

"What you need, fam?" Biz asked him.

"Two hundred of loud and an eight ball."

"I got you, homie," Biz replied, putting his bottle on the gate as he calls Kev on the phone to come over to him.

"You got powder on you; right? My nigga right here needs a couple of grams," Biz asked Kev.

"Yeah," Kev replies as he digs in his pocket.

With no hesitation and as quick and smooth as the best of them, S's gun is in the middle of Biz's forehead and Macho's gun is on Kev. A chill runs through Biz's body as he stares S in the eyes. Sweat builds up on his forehead as the feel of the hard steel placed on his head makes him nervous.

"Both of y'all give homie…" he nods in Horse's direction, "ya chains and your money; don't make me kill y'all," S said, observing everything around him while looking at Biz through the corner of his eye.

Biz and Kev stood frozen as Horse took the chains off of their necks and dug in their pockets. "I got everything," Horse said, taking a step back.

"You bitch ass niggas don't know who you're robbing!" Biz said, staring S dead in his eyes.

The feeling S always gets when he's about to snatch a life runs through his body; it's the feeling of power and invincibility; playing the role of God with the power to determine whether a person lives or dies due to his hands.

Before Biz tried to make his move and snatch S's gun...*Boom!* A hollow tip bullet rips through his skull; followed by five more shots that fill his chest as five shots from Macho's gun rip apart Kev's chest at the same time. The shots echo through the dark sky. The screams of women and children fill the air as garbage cans and tables are pushed over and everybody starts running in different directions off of the block to safety. A night of partying comes to an end for Gotti and his team along with the rest of the people on the block enjoying the BBQ. S, Macho and Horse make it back to the truck, hop in and pull off. Gotti and a bunch of people including King, run over to the scene. They find Biz and Kev, side by side, lying in a pool of their own blood, filled with bullet holes; both of their eyes are wide open, staring up into the dark sky.

The screams from Biz's mother and girlfriend can be heard over the crowd of people that surround the dead bodies.

"No, please, God...no! Don't do this to me. Not my baby!" Mrs. Walker screams out, dropping to the ground and holding the lifeless body of her only child and then pulling Kev's lifeless body into her arms as well.

"Where were you at?" Tasha, Biz's girlfriend says to Gotti, smacking his chest as he holds her while tears roll down his face.

"I'mma find out who did this," King said, putting his hand on Gotti's shoulder, inwardly having no remorse for what he ordered to be done. He looks into Gotti's eyes noticing the pain and he could immediately tell that Gotti had nothing to do with killing Mac, as the sounds of police sirens, ambulances and helicopters enclose on D.S. block.

Sitting in Roses Coffee Shop with the TV on mute while the smell of cigars and cognac linger in the air... Haze, Mel and Tone wait for Flush to finish talking on the phone.

*****

"Everything went good, just the way we wanted it to," Flush said after hanging up his phone.

"Good," Haze said, smacking his hands together and getting up from the table with a smile on his face. The feeling of relief runs through him as he looks at the faces of everyone at the table and notices they are happy with the outcome also. "Let's get out of here and hit the Green

House up. Turn everything off and set the alarm," Haze said, walking out the door.

*****

As he does every morning at 6:00 a.m., wearing his Polo bathrobe and sitting on his couch, King drinks a cup of coffee and reads the *48 Laws Of Power* from front to back or until Nicole runs into the living room begging for cereal and refusing to let him finish reading. His daughter's need for attention usually brings the end to his morning reading ritual, but not this time; his morning read is not interrupted by Nicole, it's interrupted by a text from Nando Sanchez.

Meet me at noon; 67th Street and Roosevelt Avenue. El Sito Restaurant, the text reads.

I'll be there, King sends a text back and closes his book.

A smile appears on King's face as he watches Kia in her bathrobe. He could sit and watch her all day, every day. She brings a sense of calmness to him even without trying. She's beautiful, especially in the morning. Her satin bathrobe is tied loosely at her waist and hair is wrapped in a bun as she walks in to the living room and sits down next to him.

"This is the video montage of Mac that Asia and I made for the wake," she said, handing him a DVD.

Putting the DVD in, King sits back down on the couch and watches the video footage of vacations in different countries all over the world. The pictures bring back memories of the times they had together. As the footage plays of Mac's wedding in Monaco, King's heart takes a deep hit as he watches Mac teaching Nicole how to dance.

"Nicole had the time of her life out there. She didn't want to leave," Kia said as she stared at the DVD along with King. She had a slight smile on her face, but sorrow in her voice.

"I know. I didn't wanna leave either; it's fucking beautiful out there. They had one of the most beautiful weddings that I had ever been to. How's Asia holding up?" he asked.

"Not good. After the funeral she's moving to a house Mac bought her in Orlando. She said that the memories here are too painful. She showed me pictures of it and the house is big as hell. Between me and you, she found a stash of money that Mac had hidden in the house;

five million in cash, five million in bearer bonds and a list of offshore bank accounts holding fifty million in her name. She's crazy rich, thanks to Mac. He made sure she would be taken care of if he wasn't around."

"That's good. I told her to talk to his accountant, Daniel Schwartz, and check his investments in the stock market. There's at least a hundred million dollars moving around in there too; probably more."

"What the fuck? Are you serious?" she asked.

"Yeah, Mac made a lot of money throughout the years and I'm talking…a lot," he replied.

"Damn, I didn't know he made that much money."

"Yes, he did; he was just smooth about not letting everyone know just how much money he was holding'," he replied, grabbing her by the shoulder and pulling her close to him. The scent of fresh vanilla from her hair engulfed him. They both laughed watching the video montage as footage of Mac and King arguing with each other over who was going to jump out of an air plane first flashed across the screen. It was a memory of the time they went sky diving in Vegas, and a glimpse of the depth of the friendship he shared with Mac.

CHAPTER 5

"Only real legends go out like this."
~*Flush*

Driving up Roosevelt Avenue on a beautiful Sunday afternoon, King notices El Sito restaurant and makes a right on 67th Street, finding a parking spot right behind a white Lamborghini. *It's hot as hell out here*, he said to himself, turning the corner and walking toward the restaurant. The smell of roast pork and rice and beans resonates in the air in front of the restaurant as King opens the door.

"Hello, señor. How are you doing today?" the beautiful Cuban hostess said to him.

"I'm doing fine, ma'am," King replied, removing his black shades. "I'm meeting somebody; as a matter of fact, I see him over there," he said as a short, muscular-built Spanish man in a blue suit waves him over to a table in the back of the restaurant.

King followed the hostess to the back seating area where Nando and three of his bodyguards are drinking Tequila and watching the soccer game between Mexico and Puerto Rico being shown on a 70-inch flat screen TV hanging above the bar.

"King...my man, what's going on?" Nando said as he stands up and shakes King's hand. "Have a seat. There's coffee, food, Tequila...help yourself to whatever you want."

"Coffee will be good," King replied as he sits down and pours himself a cup.

"Mierda *(Spanish for, shit)*!" A tall and slim, brown-skinned man in a brown suit screams out as he stands up. Disgusted with the way the soccer game is turning out, he stops watching the game and walks over to Nando's table, taking a seat.

"King, I would like you to meet Mr. Felix Lopez, my business partner. He wanted to meet the person that was replacing our good friend, Mac...so he wanted to join us today," Nando said, as the two shake hands and they begin talking.

After a long hour of talking business, eating and drinking, as he walks out of the restaurant, King realizes the moment he had been waiting for, for the past two years has finally arrived – the opportunity to be the richest drug dealer in New York City. No other drug dealer in any of the five boroughs in the city that King knew of dealt with the Rayon Cartel; only him.

*****

"This son of a bitch is eating alone on a Sunday afternoon. Damn, they must make some good Cuban food," Agent Bauer said to Agent Mackey as they sit in a black Tahoe directly across the street from the restaurant.

"I guess so," Agent Mackey replied with his green eyes fixated on a short, Spanish woman walking past the car.

"He parked around the corner, so I gotta make a U-turn. What the…you gotta be fucking kidding me!"

"What's wrong, Sam?" Agent Mackey asked.

"That's Nando Sanchez and Felix Lopez walking out of the restaurant," Agent Bauer replied.

"Oh, shit…it's them. Fuck the food, King must have had a meeting with them in there. His connect is the fucking, Rayon Cartel!" Agent Mackey said.

"Wow, fuck King…I'm following them!" Agent Bauer said, making a U-turn.

Following Nando's white Lamborghini and a black Mercedes Benz on the Grand Central Parkway for two miles, Agent Bauer notices that they are about to get off at the LaGuardia Airport exit. He becomes frustrated because he thought they were going to lead him to one of their hideouts in New York. Exiting the highway and driving through to the departing flights section of the airport, Nando and Felix both get out of the Lambo and nod their heads to the driver of the black Mercedes Benz as they walk into the airport where their private plane, which was prepared to head to Mexico, is waiting for them.

*****

"Where the fuck is Tone? I told him to be here at 5:00," King said out loud as he, Haze, Mel and Flush sat at the tables outside the coffee shop watching a basketball game being played across the street.

"He was at Asia's house the last time I spoke to him," Mel said.

Pulling out what looks just like a phone from his pocket and placing it on the table, King then turns on the radio frequency scrambler. It intercepts, scrambles, and distorts any wiretap signals picked up by the device within a two hundred-yard radius.

"Fuck it, if he is with her, she probably gave him all the details already. Mac's wake is Tuesday, and the last viewing and the funeral are on Wednesday. Everything is already taken care of: transportation, flowers, the obituary, food for the repast and the suits for all the crew. Y'all gotta pick up your suits tomorrow at Romo's in midtown. He wants all of you there at 10:00 a.m., the major thing I wanted to talk to y'all about was the drop taking place on Thursday; a ton of dope," King said.

"Now that's what I'm talking about," Mel said, folding his hands together and getting excited about the possibility of all the money they were about to make.

"I got two stash houses and two labs already set up for us, all high-tech shit inside and outside; equipment and surveillance. I want everybody there when it comes in so y'all can meet these people 'cause y'all are going to be dealing with them from now on," King told them.

"No problem," Haze replied and everyone else nodded their heads.

"Were ready to flood Long Island City, all of Astoria, and all of Woodside and Lefrak City. I'm still waiting on phone calls from the Haitian Unit in Corona, and Zane, the head of the White Lions in Flushing. My dudes out in Jamaica are ready; but first we gotta get rid of Wise and Mace and then we could set up out there," King stated, observing the smiles on everyone's faces as he took a sip of coffee.

"All of these niggas think that since Mac is gone, they gonna run they own shit now; motherfuckers are crazy. We're about to take over all of Queens and then the rest of New York. It's time to *Paint The City Red*, my niggas," King said as he takes a deep breath and stares into the sun shining above them.

*****

Standing in the living room, looking out the window at the Manhattan skyline and East river, King can't stop thinking about Mac. He puts on a black Fedora that matches his black Gucci suit and hard bottoms. He can't help thinking about the fact that he is about to see his face for the last time before burying him. *It was all good just a week ago; this shit doesn't make any sense,* he says to himself as he walks to the bedroom to check on Kia and Nicole to see if they are ready. The sounds of cartoon voices come through the speakers of the TV as King stands at the door of the bedroom and watches as the two most important people in his life finish getting ready.

As Kia is fixing Nicole's dress, looking out the corner of her eye into the mirror, she sees King leaning up against the wall watching them; she can see the pain in his face. It's the same pain she saw when he lost both of his parents when he was seventeen. His parents, Chris and Maria Johnson, died in a car crash on route 84 in New Jersey while coming back from a weekend getaway. A man driving a GMC Yukon had a heart attack while he was driving and ended up sideswiping King's parents' car; causing them to crash into two other cars and then flip over two times. They were both D.O.A. at the hospital. It was a hard time for King being that young and losing both of his parents at the same time; but Kia was there for him and helped him get through it.

"You okay, babe?" Kia asked, standing up and walking over to him. She looked into his hazel eyes and ran her finger across his thin, neatly-trimmed goatee. She wished she could take away her man's pain.

"Yeah, I'm good. Y'all ready?"

"Yes, we are. Let's go, Nicole...time to see Uncle Mac."

"Good, now I can tell him what I want for my birthday, even though he already knows," she innocently replied, following behind her parents out of the room.

Close to a thousand people showed up to Mac's final viewing at Ortiz Funeral Home on 35th Street and Broadway in Astoria, Queens. Family members, friends and business associates crowded the inside, as well as the outside of the funeral home. The NYPD is also outside in numbers, making their presence felt to prevent any violence from happening.

"It's crazy out here; there's more people today than there was yesterday," Flush said to Tone as they both smoked cigarettes while standing in front of the funeral home. "There are at least a thousand people out here right now."

"I saw a lot of out-of-state plates too," Tone said, staring at the undercover cop car across the street.

"Mac is going out the right way with that glass-top coffin King got him," Flush said.

"It's only right," Haze said, walking up behind Flush and Tone and putting his arms around both of their shoulders. "King, just hit me up and said he is pulling up in a few. Move the cones and put them in the trunk," Haze told Tone.

"It's crazy out here," Kia said to King as they pulled up. She couldn't help staring at the crowds of people gathered on every block next to and in front of the funeral home. Cars were double parked in the streets and NYPD cars blocked off some of the blocks around the funeral home that were already too full. Damn near everybody outside was in all black.

"He was a legend in some people's eyes," King said, staring at all the different faces standing outside. Young, old, family and friends – all came to pay their respects to Mac. King smiled thinking that one day he would face the same fate.

"What's a legend, daddy?" Nicole asked.

"Someone who will be remembered forever; that's what a legend is."

As they park in front of the funeral home, King sees that all eyes are focused in his direction. Knowing that everyone is waiting for him to step out of the car, a chill runs through his body as he unbuckles Nicole's seatbelt and sees a smile on her face.

"There's a lot of people looking at you, daddy," Nicole said, staring at her father.

"They're not staring at me; they all want to see your pretty face."

As King steps out of the passenger side with Nicole, all attention is on them. All that can be heard through the air are the whispers of people as they stare. Smiles stretch across the faces of Mac's family members and those who knew what King did that night and the way he was sending Mac home.

What the fuck is going on? Why people whispering and staring as if King was the one who killed Mac? Kia said to herself as she slams the driver's side door.

"Uncle Flush, you owe me ten dollars. You thought I forgot, huh?" Nicole said giving him a hug.

"Everything good?" King asked, giving everybody a pound and a hug.

"Yeah, it's all good," Mel replied.

"That glass-top coffin is serious, fam; we sending him out right," Flush said to King.

Nodding his head in an agreement with Flush, "It's a sad day for Queensbridge, but he's in a better place now," King stated.

Staring at everyone in his crew dressed in all-black, the thought of losing one of them crosses King's mind. He realizes from this moment on, life will change for all of them and this won't be the last time they will be dressed like this standing in front of a funeral home; because some will make it and some won't.

"Let's go upstairs," Haze said, opening the door for everyone.

Making their way through the packed lobby and up the stairs to the overcrowded hallway, King and Kia are greeted by Asia and her parents. Pain, stress and exhaustion all show on Asia's beautiful face. Thinking about Mac, not being able to sleep, and figuring out where she would go from this point on, has taken a toll her and it is written all over her face for all to see.

"How are you holding up?" King asked, giving Asia a long hug and kiss on the cheek.

"The best I can," she replied, wiping her eye with a white cloth.

"We're all here for you; whatever you need, just let us know."

"I know, King. I know. Let's go inside to say goodbye," Asia replied as she grabs Nicole's hand and they all walk in.

Once again, all eyes land upon King as he enters the room which is packed to capacity with family members, friends and gangstas from all over New York. Dozens upon dozens of sympathy and religious bouquets of different colored flowers that relatives and close friends of Mac brought in are placed on tables and wherever they could find room to place them. But what stands out the most are the flowers King purchased. Six, standing-spray, rose-colored, garden heart flowers, each six feet tall are placed in the front of the room. The reason King bought six of the standing flowers was because he always remembered it was Mac's favorite number. All six of the six-feet-tall flowers surround Mac's coffin which King had custom-made in China. It was a luxurious European-style, titanium coffin with a glass top. King wanted to send Mac out in style because he knew Mac would do the same for him; so he had no problem dropping $40,000 on a casket for the person he called his big brother. Two 60-inch flat screen TVs are hanging from the ceiling and located on both sides of the coffin. The video montage that Kia and Asia made with pictures and video footage of Mac through the years plays in the background.

The people in line waiting to say their goodbyes to Mac allow King, Kia and Nicole to go ahead of them to the front to say their goodbyes. King stands by and watches as Kia cries, holding Mac's hand and saying a prayer to him. *Damn, my nigga Mac is gone,* King said to himself, holding back the tears from falling down his face. Kia gets up and walks back to King, giving him a hug and a kiss. Sweetly she whispers, *I love you* to him in his ear. Her words make a difficult situation just a little bit easier to bear.

A smile appears on King's face as he stands in front of the casket. The same way it did when he stood in front of his parents' caskets years ago. Mac lies in the casket wearing a cream-colored Armani suit, his favorite Rolex, and a pinky ring and platinum chain. His hair is freshly tapered up with his waves spinning as always, and his gray goatee is neatly trimmed. King had slipped Mac's favorite barber extra money on the side to get him to freshen up his look instead of the beautician that the funeral home provides. He wanted to make sure that Mac looked as good in death as he did while living. He knew Mac wouldn't have it any other way. Staring at Mac, memories replay in King's mind of all the good times they had and especially the trip they took to Colombia and how they almost got kidnapped hanging out in Medellin.

"You look at peace, my nigga. Everybody came out for you. Family, friends and even niggas you had beef with back in the days came to pay their respect. I know you in a better place now. You told me to do it bigger than you did. That was one of the last things you told me that night. I'll always be there for Asia; she doesn't have to worry about anything. I promise you," King said under his breath.

"Daddy, can I see Uncle Mac?" Nicole asked, standing behind him.

"Yeah, come on," King said as she steps onto the stool and stares at Mac lying peacefully in the casket.

"When is he gonna wake up?" she asked, with a concerned look on her face.

"Not for a long time, babygirl."

"Why? Okay...so he's gonna wake up for my birthday party; right? Uncle Mac promised me a trip to the zoo and some ice cream from Bella's. He knows I don't want to miss that."

Everybody watching can't help but smile and wipe the tears from their eyes as they looked at Nicole's adorable facial expressions when she talked.

"He won't be able to, but I'll take you. Now, let's say goodbye to Uncle Mac; other people are waiting in line to see him too."

"Okay," she leans into the casket. "Bye Uncle Mac, I'll see you at my party. I know you will wake up by then. We're gonna have pizza and fun," she whispered into his ear like they always used to do to each other.

"One king leaves and another steps right in his shoes," Agent Mackey said to his partner as they stand on the corner, across the street, watching King and his crew carry Mac's coffin outside to the hearse.

"It's only a matter of time before they fall, Mackey. You know that," Agent Donaldson replied.

"Fall...he hasn't even gotten started yet. Fuck what Bauer be talking about," he takes a pull from his cigar. "I put it to you like this...imagine Carlo Gambino and Bumpy Johnson wrapped into one person. That's the kind of monster we are facing."

As King drops the top to the phantom, Flush –who's sitting shotgun – puts on Mac's favorite album of all time; "Reasonable Doubt." As the hearse pulls off, fifty cars follow behind it headed toward Queensbridge. Making a right on to 40th Avenue from 21st Street, the hearse starts its tour of the hood. King had barricades set up and the streets shut down along the route they were going to take. It's the last time Mac's body will be in Queensbridge and the last time Queensbridge will feel his presence.

Driving down 40th Avenue, onlookers wave and put their fists in the air saluting Mac as the fifty-car convoy passes by. Driving up to Monte's lounge, King stares at the crowds of people standing in front. People are lighting candles, leaving flowers and screaming Mac's name as the hearse makes a left in between 10th Street and Vernon.

Everybody starts running through the 40th side of 10th Street and up to the hill where the rest of the neighborhood is waiting to say goodbye.

The hill is so crowded that people are now standing on the rooftops of stores on both sides of the street. At least a hundred police officers and a bunch of captains are on the hill to make sure no violence erupts because of the unpredictable atmosphere of the colliding types of people in the area. Bottles of Rose Moet and Hennessey are being waved around in the air as everybody is wearing white t-shirts that Haze had made for the people in the neighborhood to wear. The shirts read, *Rest In Peace Mac*, in bold orange letters and have a picture of Mac on the front and back of the shirt.

The lyrics from the song, "Can I Live" blast through the speakers of King's phantom as the hearse and the convoy drives slowly through the hill and then stops in front of the candy store.

Chills run through King's body as he stares at close to a thousand people wearing a t-shirt with a picture of Mac on it. There were people standing on the rooftops of stores and some were hanging out of their apartment windows screaming Mac's name. Little kids were waving at the hearse and tears were drenching the faces of a lot of people.

"This shit is crazy, fam; only real legends go out like this," Flush said to King as they watch the out pouring of love the people have for Mac.

Smoking a cigar and taking in the moment, King can't help but think, *What's it gonna be like when I die? Will I be celebrated the same way, and will it be anything like this?*

The hearse and the fifty car convoy heads out of Queensbridge on its way to New Calvary Cemetery in Woodside, Queens to lay Tyler Hampton, aka Mac, to rest.

INTERMISSION

The large steel doors of a warehouse open in Glendale, Queens as King and his crew watch two white Salvation Army vans back in. Opening the back doors of the vans and seeing what was inside was the moment they'd been waiting for. Inside the vans were two thousand pounds of pure dope, packed inside cardboard boxes. It was the first step in their process of King's plan.

Over the next year, King and his crew did whatever it took to take over Queens and start branching out to the other boroughs. Since Mac died, a lot of the crews that used to work for him thought they were gonna run their own hoods and not work for King; they underestimated King and what he was willing to do. He started out by taking over Jamaica, Queens. In order to do that, he had Wise and Mace – who ran Southside and Hollis, Queens – murdered at the West Indian Day Parade in Brooklyn in broad daylight. He had two Spanish women, dressed like cops, gun them down on Flatbush Avenue and Winthrop Street. He knew that a statement as bold as that would have the streets talking. Then there was the war he waged against the White Lions, a Chinese gang in Flushing, Queens. After

King had seven members of their gang killed in just two weeks, Zane, the leader of the White Lions surrendered and started working for King. And then there was the Halloween massacre that took place at Club Rebel in Corona, Queens. King had his cousin S, and his crew – The Hit Squad – kill the two leaders of the Haitian Unit along with four of their soldiers in the club on Halloween night.

Within a year of working with the Rayon Cartel, King and his crew had made more money than they ever saw in their lives before that time. Flooding the streets of New York with tons of dope that they called Dream and a shitload of weed made King a multi-millionaire. Moving out of their condo in Long Island City, Queens, King, Kia and Nicole moved into a beautiful custom built eight-million-dollar home in the East Williston District of Old Westbury, New York. It's tucked away in the woods and only thirty minutes from the hood. Haze and Flush followed suit and bought newly built lofts in Long Island City, Queens; and Tone and Mel bought houses in Hackensack, New Jersey. Riding around New York in foreign cars, buying million-dollar houses and lofts, wearing more jewelry and the murder rate going up fifty percent in Queens from the year before, made King and his crew the FBI's number one target in New York.

CHAPTER 6

"It's not about the money Haze, it's the power."
~King

A little over a year later

Thursday, November 1
Bronx, NY

Strike two! It's fifty degrees and the smell of beer, hot dogs and pretzels fill the air on a November night in the Bronx at Yankee Stadium. It's game five of the World Series and the Yankees are playing the San Francisco Giants. The Yankees have a 2-1 lead in the bottom of the fifth inning. The stadium is packed like it always is during this time of the year. Sitting behind the visiting team's dugout along the third baseline in the seats Mac owned and that they used to sit in together, is King. He is wearing his A-Rod jersey over a blue Yankee hoodie and a Yankee fitted. King took over the season ticket plan once Mac passed away. He still enjoys coming to the stadium, even though he comes by himself unless he brings Nicole with him.

114

"God damn! My friend, can you please move your arm? You're killing me over here. I can't enjoy the game 'cause you all up in my space," a light-skinned Spanish man said in a loud tone to someone sitting next to him.

"What you want me to do? I didn't make these seats so fucking small. If you want more room, you should have got a seat in the bleachers," the man replied.

"I should have gotten a seat in the bleachers? Are you fucking serious? They should have sold your ass a standing room only ticket. You know damn well you're too fat to be sitting in these seats!" the Spanish man replied.

King lets out a slight laugh watching the two men go back and forth seated a couple of seats away from him to his left. "My man in the suit, there's an empty seat here. My friend is not showing up so you can sit here," King told the light-skinned Spanish man wearing a light gray Tom Ford suit.

"Thank you for the seat, my friend. I appreciate it," the man said with a Spanish accent.

"No problem."

"Let me get you a drink for your courtesy. Do you drink Cognac?"

"Yeah, that's cool," King replied, analyzing the Spanish man with a clean-shaven face and shiny, wavy black hair who was digging in his jacket pocket.

Pulling out his cell phone, the man makes a call to usher staff and orders two drinks to be brought to him.

"Why you sitting in these seats if you got VIP service?" King asked him.

"Man...fuck a suite; I like sitting out here with the regular fans. I love the feeling and the smell of the stadium. My name is Luis Beltre by the way," the man said, extending his hand out.

"I'm King," he announces as they both shake hands.

"Mr. King, it's a pleasure to finally meet you. I heard a lot of good things about you."

King's left eyebrow arched up and he moved his right hand toward his waist, gripping his 40 cal Sig Sauer. "Excuse me. What you know about me?"

"Enough. I admire the way you handle business and the fact that you're a family man. I see how much you love your daughter and the way you and her bond when you bring her here with you sometimes. I have two daughters and one son. Family is everything, my friend."

Anger grows inside of King as the usher brings them their drinks and Mr. Beltre continues to speak.

"See, King…I know what you do for a living. I'm not the Feds by the way, just in case you were thinking that. The people you deal with…" Mr. Beltre says as he touches his own face, alluding to his skin color and ethnic background, "…won't be around too long to continue doing business with you."

Clackkk!!!

"It's gone, baby!" King screamed out as he and the rest of the people in the stadium stand up and celebrate a homerun hit by the Yankees first baseman. "Listen, I don't know what you're telling me this for, but if you have problems in your life, you need to take care of them. It makes you a better person and you'll feel better," King said to him with a bit of sarcasm in his words.

"Indeed. A wise man said the same exact thing to me before. He used to sit in this same seat I'm sitting in. I used to talk with him some times; a couple of years ago when he used to come here. I haven't seen him in a while," he stands up. "Life sometimes puts you on a path you don't wanna take. So you have to find a way to deal with it, adjust and you'll make it to the end of the road. It was a pleasure meeting you, Mr. Johnson. We'll be doing business together very soon," Mr. Beltre assured him and then walked away.

How the fuck is that nigga in this country; just sitting here at a Yankee game without a care in the world, King said to himself, shaking his head and feeling a little irritated. He somehow knew that the man he just met would do anything to get what he wants.

*****

Luis Ivan Beltre, aka El Monstruo, is the most violent drug lord in all of Puerto Rico. The forty-three year old is the head of the La Perla Cartel based out of San Juan. He stands 5'8" with a muscular build, shiny wavy black hair and he always has a clean-shaven face. His net worth is listed around five-hundred million dollars; which is a result of his reign over the distribution of dope and cocaine that's transported from Puerto Rico into the United States. He took control of the drug trade in Puerto Rico five years ago by going to war with the rival Cartels from Mexico; mainly with the Ciudad Cartel trying to control the drug trade in Puerto Rico.

The media gave him the nick name, El Monstruo (The Monster) because of the thousands of murders he was responsible for. His strong political ties with the Puerto Rico government and America seem to keep him off of the

World's Most Wanted list for some reason. His lifestyle inspires the young kids of Puerto Rico. The way he dresses – wearing expensive Tom Ford suits and YSL clothing, the foreign cars he drives, all the money he makes, the businesses he owns, the schools and playgrounds he had built for the kids, and the sports leagues and charities he sponsors – all add money to his home town. Then there's the four-hundred-acre estate he owns, which is guarded by his army and has the most high-tech surveillance system money can buy. The estate includes a lavish forty-million dollar mansion, a baseball field, mini waterpark, a mini movie theater, a heliport and the list goes on.

Luis Ivan Beltre was born and raised in the slums of La Perla; the most dangerous part of San Juan, Puerto Rico. He was raised by a single mother who had to work two jobs, making just enough money to pay rent and put food on the table for him and his two younger brothers because his father was never there for them. It was easy for the young Luis to get involved in a life of crime; having no money, his mother never being home because she had to work all the time, and a father who abandoned them.

Luis and his younger brothers, Juan and Jose, started off controlling the marijuana trade in San Juan and Bayamon. All marijuana sold in those two towns or transported out, came from them. Within no time, their operation grew bigger and they recruited enough soldiers to control the marijuana trade in all of Puerto Rico. They became multi-millionaires and lived a lifestyle more lavish than the older drug kingpins that controlled the dope and coke trade in Puerto Rico. But Luis wanted more money and more power.

He and his brothers waged a war against the two major drug kingpins in Puerto Rico at the time; Alex Fuentes and Raul Solis who both worked for the Ciudad Cartel from Mexico. The war campaign only lasted four days, because Luis got information on Alex Fuentes' second family – a wife and two sons – who lived in Miami, Florida. He had their car blown up with them in it as the mother was driving the two sons to school. As soon as Alex got word of what happened, he tried to move his first family – a wife and daughter – who lived with him in Fajardo, Puerto Rico into hiding in Mexico. But, by the time he got home to get them, they were already kidnapped and he was killed as soon as he walked into his daughter's bedroom to look for her.

Hearing what had happened to Alex Fuentes and both of his families on just the 4th day of the war Luis Beltre and his brothers started, Raul Solis wanted no parts of it and surrendered; giving up his drug operations and moving with his family to Argentina. The leader of the Ciudad Cartel was furious and waged a war against Luis and his brothers that lasted a year, and Luis and his brothers eventually won and gained full control of Puerto Rico. Years later, after a couple thousand dead bodies and hundreds of millions of dollars richer, Luis has a new problem now. Hector Santiago and his Rayon Cartel from Sonora, Mexico.

As the rain pours down outside on a Saturday afternoon, *CNN* plays on the 70-inch flat screen TV inside Roses coffee shop. King and Haze are sitting down at a table next to the window, talking business as usual as customers come in and out of the store, purchasing freshly-baked pastries and coffee. King renovated the shop a year ago, giving it a more inviting and friendlier feel to it than the eerie and dark mafia-looking social club it felt like before. Pictures of great Yankee moments along with pictures of beautiful art work hang on the beige walls throughout the shop. The black round coffee tables where replaced with light brown ones and a large display case for the pastries was built on the opposite side of the coffee station.

"You won't believe who was sitting next to me at the Yankee game the other day," King told Haze.

"Who, Giuliani?"

"Nah, nigga...Luis Beltre, EL Monstruo. The motherfucker has been watching us. I don't know how long, but he's been watching."

"Jesus Christ. He knows who supplies us then. So you know what he wants."

"Yeah, I know. He's about to take Rayon to war. Which means we're stuck in the middle of their bullshit," King replied, staring at the TV.

"Every single one of those Cartels in South America makes hundreds of millions of dollars a year, but they're still going to war with each other. The shit never made any sense to me. They are all getting money out there and Luis Beltre runs all of Puerto Rico; he's probably worth a couple hundred million," Haze said, shaking his head.

"It's not about the money, Haze; it's about the power," King told him.

"Did you tell Nando yet? 'Cause what's about to happen is gonna slow us down."

"Yeah, I told him. He said he don't give a fuck about La Perla, the Rayon is bigger. So he and Hector feel they're gonna win the war. Wow, look who finally shows up," King said, as Tone, Mel and Flush walk through the door.

"Speaking of the devil," Haze said, grabbing the remote and putting the volume up on the TV. "Look what they're showing on TV now," he says as *CNN* reports a story from Mexico where six members of the Rayon Cartel were beheaded on a live internet stream.

"As long as them motherfuckers keep that bullshit in their countries and not Queens, I don't give a fuck what they do; they can kill each other all they want," King said, getting up and lighting a Lano Estate cigar as he walks to his office in the back and his crew follows him. King and Kia started their own cigar line six months ago, called Lano Estate. Their products are made in the Dominican Republic and have been selling out in cigar shops around New York.

Watching as King takes a seat behind his desk, Tone can see that King is irritated about something 'cause his eyes turned narrow when he looked at Haze. "Haze, we got a shipment coming in this upcoming Friday the ninth, out in Jamaica. Troy is gonna be there, but I want you there too. How we doing with the other thing…the Bronx?" King asked, leaning back in his leather chair, waiting for Haze's response.

"Nobody has seen him around. I'm on it though, don't worry about it," Haze replied.

"Listen, it's been a month now and I don't care that he's your cousin. You fronted him four joints and now he's nowhere to be found. The motherfucker ran off with our shit and I'm not taking that loss. So find him ASAP or pay that bill!" King told him in a dark tone.

"I'll find him and if he doesn't have the money, I'll kill him!" Haze replied, grabbing a pool stick as he and Tone got ready to play a game. Even though Haze is a smooth-dressing ladies' man and has a Wall Street style swagger, he's just as ruthless and manipulative as King; killing without remorse and using anyone for his benefit.

"Family will fuck you over the most; if you show them too much love they'll take advantage of you every chance they get," King said, pulling out his ledger from his desk drawer.

"They most definitely will," Mel stated in a Haitian accent, taking a seat on the couch.

"So far this month we pulled in twelve million. That's three million short of what we made the last month. The majority of that loss comes from the Skillman crew. They're down seventy-seven percent this month and their numbers have been going down for the past six months,"

King said to everyone; waiting for someone to give him an explanation as to why.

"I meet with Danny Boy (the new leader of the Skillman crew), yesterday at his barbershop and he told me shit been slow out there. He said they haven't been bringing in the same money they used to when J-Cash ran shit. His mouth changes with the wind. I think he's lying if you ask me. There's too much money out there, so he might turn out to be a problem," Flush informed King.

"He still thinks we allowed Gotti to kill J-Cash?" King asked.

"Of course…even though we all told him we didn't have anything to do with it, he doesn't believe us and he's not gonna let that go. That was his cousin," Flush replied.

King could care less if Danny Boy was mad that his cousin was dead. J-Cash didn't wanna work for King anymore because he was getting his dope at a cheaper price from a connect in Washington Heights and he decided to cut King out. So, King told Gotti he got word that J-Cash and two of his soldiers were the ones that killed Biz and Kev. Then he gave Gotti J-Cash's information. As he leaned back in his chair and stared at Tone and Haze play pool, King reminisces about that Valentine's Day.

Eight months earlier

Tuesday, February 14 8:30 p.m.
Bronx, N.Y

It's a beautiful night at The Sea Shore Restaurant on City Island in the Bronx. J-Cash and his wife, Rosalyn, are celebrating their two-year wedding anniversary. The happy couple is enjoying the beginning of a night of fun that he had planned for her.

Parked outside the restaurant in a black, tinted-out, Cadillac GTV, waiting for J-Cash and his wife to walk out of the restaurant, is Gotti. He does not say a word; he just waits patiently as King sits next to him smoking a cigar. Parked up the block in a black Audi, just in case anything goes wrong, is Hoffa.

"The food was good, baby. I've been up here so many times, but I never came in this restaurant. I like it; something about the atmosphere seems perfect to me. This is the new spot for us," Rosalyn said to J-Cash as she leaned in close to him.

"Most definitely, but I got something else planned for us in the city. You gonna love it," he said, grabbing her hand and rubbing it gently.

"What? You going all out tonight; I can't wait to see what it is."

"Trust me, you gonna love it," he replied as the waiter walks over to the table and hands him the check.

They putting on their coats, getting ready to head out. The words are uttered over a walkie talkie from inside the restaurant to the other walkie talkies.

"Copy that," Gotti replied as he gripped his 357. Magnum narrowed his eyes and kept his focus on the front door of the restaurant.

Walking out the restaurant as Rosalyn has her arm wrapped around J-Cash's arm and her head on his shoulder, a look of concern appears on his face. As a man in all-black walks past him shouting curse words in the air, arguing with himself while looking in J-Cash's direction. Feeling a little uncomfortable, J puts his hand on his burner just in case the estranged man tries something.

"What the fuck is wrong with that nigga? He needs to leave them drugs alone for real," J-Cash said to his wife. She just nodded her head in agreement.

127

Appearing on the right side of J-Cash from behind the stonewall alongside the entrance of the restaurant, dressed in all-black and extending his right arm holding a stainless steel 44. Magnum is Gotti's best hitter; Drop.

Not being able to hear anything as if she was deaf and feeling warm water being thrown in her face, Rosalyn pauses and shakes her head. The smell of gunpowder and burned hair overwhelms her. As she wipes her face and opens her eyes, she notices that both of her hands are covered with blood. She looks down and sees her husband – the father of her four kids – lay out in front of her with half of his head gone and his brains pasted on the pavement.

Dropping to her knees with her heart racing at a hundred miles a minute, Rosalyn tries to wake her husband up as the staff of the restaurant rush outside to the aid of the couple, after calling the police.

Running up the block and hopping into the black Audi that Hoffa was waiting in, is Drop and the estranged man J-Cash had been focused on outside the restaurant.

"Aight, he's a wrap," Gotti said to King as he pulls off satisfied with the outcome.

"What the fuck did Drop use on that nigga? Jesus Christ!" King said as he takes a pull from his cigar.

Snapping back to reality from the sound of Tone slamming the pool stick against the table, King watches as Flush counts a stack of money he had gotten from Fatal. Thinking of the money Fatal has brought in over the past year brings a smile to King's face. Fatal has made close to four million dollars off of running King's weed operation in Long Island City, Astoria and other parts of Queens. A young legend in the making is what King calls him whenever he talks about the young Fatal. Getting up and putting on his dark green leather gator-print coat and grabbing his keys and a large black duffel bag, King lets everyone know he's gonna head home to get some rest. He's been on his grind non-stop and it's taking a toll on him.

Exiting the Grand Central Parkway and driving down Bacon Road, the fifteen-foot high, black steel gates at the main entrance open as King enters his estate and drives up the mixed stoned driveway to his custom built eight-million-dollar home. It's a beautiful ten-thousand square foot Colonial, two-story home with four oversized bedrooms, four baths, a movie room in the basement, a large oversized all-white open concept kitchen, and a breathtaking living room with thirty-foot-high ceilings. It's breath taking even at first glance. Then there's the two oversized his and hers walk-in closets in the master bedroom. Kia's side is filled with everything you could find on Madison Avenue and King's side is filled with the most expensive designer suits, clothing, shoes and custom-made sneakers known to man. And last, but not least, there's the 2,500 square foot backyard that has a 700 square foot swimming pool along with a jacuzzi and a 300 square foot patio for entertainment and barbecuing; their home if fitting of royalty, which is exactly what King and Kia are to the streets.

"Business is going good; even though I had to fire the manager of the salon in Forrest Hills. The bitch was trying to steal my customers away from me to go to her sister's salon behind my back. She thought I wouldn't find out. That bitch is crazy," Kia said to her sister, Lisa, as they sat downstairs in the movie room of her house.

"Good, 'cause I never liked her ugly ass anyway. She always had an attitude with me every time I went in there. I told you I used to see the way she would look at King when he would stop by," Lisa replied. "I think she got it bad for him."

"Well, that bitch is gone now. She can take her trifling ass to her sister's shop. No love lost here."

"When are y'all gonna get married, anyway? Ain't it time for him to put a ring on it 'cause, y'all not getting any younger," Lisa asked, watching her younger sister's whole demeanor change.

"Whenever he's ready; I'm not going to rush him. I don't need a ring to know that King loves me. We are happy where we at right now; everything is good," Kia replied, shifting her eyes to the movie on the 100-inch projection screen.

Looking at her sister's calm face, Lisa knows Kia is lying and really wants to get married soon. She can tell that Kia is just scared to push King into it because she does not know if he's ready or not and she doesn't want to pressure him.

"I'm just saying…it's been ten years and counting, girl. He better do something before I have to have words with him," Lisa said.

Sitting in his custom-built stash room inside of his walk-in closet, King puts some of his weekly profit inside of his Fort Knox-Guardian 7251 safe. Millions of dollars, two M-16s, four military-issued handguns and a bunch of jewelry sit inside of the stainless steel, bomb and fireproof safe.

"Now that's 3.8 cash I got here and there's 3.3 in the Manhattan crib and 1.5 in the PA crib. So, that's 8.6 total in cash in the cribs. Now, I got 20.2 in the bank and 10.7 tied up in businesses and stocks. So, that's 30.9 total for bank and stocks. Then, there's 15.2 in expenses. Damn, 54.7 million...in only a year and change," King said, reading through his ledger.

"Daddy, where are you? You were supposed to teach me how to make spaghetti and meatballs," Nicole screams out loud, walking up the stairs toward his room.

"I'm right here, babygirl. I didn't forget about that."

Walking into his room, her eyes widen as she sees her father sitting on a chair in the closet in front of the safe counting money.

"Come here," he said, watching as she walks in with a curious look on her face. He places her on his lap.

"How much money you got in there? Is it a lot?" she asked, staring into his eyes and playing with his goatee.

"Not that much...just a couple hundred dollars probably."

"What? You trying to tell me that you only have a few hundred dollars in this big safe? Stop teasing me, daddy. Even I can see there's way more in there than that.

I know what's really in there," she said, staring at the smirk on his face.

"What's in there then…since you know it all?"

"My Christmas presents. You're hiding them behind the money, aren't you? Yeah, you didn't think I figure that out did you? I know you better than you think I know you, daddy," she replied, getting off his lap and slapping her hands together. "So are you ready to cook now?"

Smirking and shaking his head before getting up from the chair, King responds, "Yeah, I'm ready."

"Good, 'cause I got everything ready for us. So let's go; I'm getting hungry."

"Who you talking to like that and where's your mother?" he asked, walking out of the room.

"In the movie room with Auntie Lisa, talking about you."

"Good, 'cause I don't want her stealing my recipe. You're the only one that's gonna know how to make my secret meatballs. It's an old family recipe and I'm only sharing it with my babygirl."

"I won't tell your secret, daddy. I promise."

Walking downstairs and into the beautiful, all-white, open concept kitchen, King sees that Nicole wasn't playing. She has everything he needs placed on the beige marble granite top of the humongous island counter in the middle of the kitchen.

"I see you ready to learn today."

"Yes, sir…the meatballs, sauce and spaghetti are all here…let's get it popping," she replied, putting on her *Hello Kitty* apron.

After teaching Nicole how to prepare everything, and then having her help make the sauce, meatballs, spaghetti and garlic bread, they enjoyed the big meal they made in the dining room along with Kia and Lisa.

CHAPTER 7

"I'mma put his ass away for life before I retire."

~Agent Bauer

FBI Headquarters

26 Federal Plaza - 7th floor

Manhattan, New York

"We've got something," Agent Morris said, busting through Agent Bauer's office door.

"Damn, not even a knock. You just bust through the door, Morris. What is it? Agent Bauer asked, looking at Agent Morris like he was crazy.

"I'm sorry, but we've got one of Nando's workers on the wire. He's talking about a shipment for the Jamaica crew that is ran by Troy Huggins, the man who is in this photo here with King at the Knicks game and Mr. Chow's. This is King's crew out on the Southside. We can bust these motherfuckers on this shipment and turn them."

"When is it?" Agent Bauer asked.

Paint the City Red   by Lee A. Pitts

"Friday, November 9th, at 11:00 a.m. at a storage facility off of the Belt Parkway."

"That's great fucking news. Let everyone know there's gonna be a meeting on Wednesday in the conference room about this at 10:00 a.m. on the dot," Agent Bauer instructed him.

"I got it. I'll let everyone know."

"Morris…"

"Yes, Agent Bauer?" he replied, walking back into his office.

"I want you to monitor the phone calls and computer activity of everyone you tell about this lead. I don't want any leaks coming out of this office and we wind up getting burned again."

"Not a problem, sir."

Leaning back in his chair and rubbing the top of his blond wavy hair, Agent Bauer feels relieved that he might finally have a shot at getting someone to turn against King. He also thought about the possibility of arresting members of the Rayon Cartel in the process if everything goes right. They've had good leads before, but they always fell through. It's been hard for him to get anything to stick on King. Chasing bogus leads and having people terrified to snitch on King has made Agent Bauer and the FBI's life

136

a living hell for the past year and a half. The murder rate has increased in Queens and so has the amount of drugs being brought in within the last year and a half that King has taken over.

*****

The aroma from the Spanish food could be smelled from outside, it was coming from the back of the small, Spanish bodega on McGuinness Boulevard in Greenpoint, Brooklyn. Two middle-aged Puerto Rican women have been cooking the authentic Spanish food for fifteen years out the back of the bodega. It's one of Nando Sanchez's favorite, low-key places to eat and talk business when he's in New York.

"What are we waiting for? My people were expecting the shipment this Friday," King asked Nando as they sat in the back of the bodega by themselves.

"One of my sources told me that the FBI caught one of my men on a wire talking. So we gotta hold off on that shipment for now," Nando replied as he dug his fork into a plate of beef stew and rice and beans.

"Damn! I'm running low; canceling this shipment is gonna lose us a lot of money out here," King said, getting irritated. If there's one thing besides snitches that King hates, it's losing money.

"I know, but we'll double the next shipment for you. So you'll make it back, plus more. The other thing I wanted to talk to you about was that Hector needs you to do him a favor. He wants you to handle a problem of his."

"What problem is that?" King asks as he samples the stew and beans himself.

"Sal Lombardo," Nando says nonchalantly, not missing a beat of stuffing his face.

"What? The mob boss?" King asks.

"Yes, Big Sal. We found out the big-time mob boss is an informant. We've been doing business with him for a long time and we just found out from one of our sources that he's working with the FBI. Now he's become a big problem for us. We don't know exactly what he's been giving them, but we suspect he has told them everything he knows. It can hurt our business out here, which means it hurts you and your pockets. He runs all the dope sold in Brooklyn; so it will be easier for you to expand out there now once he's gone. Hector needs this done as soon as possible."

"Unbelievable," King said, shaking his head. He knew that if he took the contract he could be in an all-out war with the mob if they found out.

"What's wrong? You didn't have a problem taking care of the other rata, (*Spanish for, rat*) that turned out to be an informant. You help us and we help you; like always. This is a very big job and Hector trusts you, that's why he wants you to handle it. We would take care of it ourselves, but we're tied up with the La Perla situation."

"This is different; but it is what it is. Just get me a list of his routes, daily routines and the address of his social club. Get that to me in a day or two and it will get done."

"King, you forgot who you're talking too," he reaches into his jacket pocket. "I already have that for you. All the information you need is right here," Nando replied, placing an envelope on the table. "Oh, yeah...I almost forgot. He wants it messy."

Everyone had mixed emotions as they sat in the basement of King's house and he informed them about the contract he had accepted on Sal Lombardo. Tone and Mel didn't have a problem with it, but Haze was the first to voice his disagreement with it and then Flush seconded him. But they both knew once King said something was going to happen, he didn't give a fuck if you disagreed with him or felt he was wrong. His orders were to be carried out, without being questioned.

*****

Thursday, November 8, 10:00 p.m.
Manhattan, New York

The house is packed on the beautiful fall night at Bella Luna Restaurant on the Upper Westside of Manhattan. It's known as one of the best Italian restaurants in the city and it's also owned by Sal Lombardo, the boss of the Lombardo crime family. The Lombardo family is the most powerful mob family in New York and the country. Standing 5'9" and weighing two hundred and fifty pounds, Big Sal at fifty-seven years old has been the boss of the family for sixteen years. The black, slicked back hair with gray wings is a feature that stands out on Sal; that, and his long hawk-like nose. He's regarded by his fellow mobsters as an old school Mafioso because of his blood-thirsty mentality and his low-key persona.

Bottles of Chateau Margaux 2003 sit on the big, round table; along with plates of veal Marsala, spaghetti carbonara, manicotti and a bunch of other dishes ordered by Sal Lombardo and five of his friends. Sal and company are celebrating the thirtieth birthday of his second cousin, Carmine Assante.

"Here's too many more birthdays and success... you're on your way up. I wish you well," Sal said to his cousin, holding his glass in the air, along with everyone else.

"Salute," everyone shouted.

As the night went on, the majority of the customers inside the restaurant are enjoying the magnificent plates they ordered made by the five-star chef. Others are still stuck in awe watching as the biggest mob boss in the country, Sal Lombardo, and his fellow mobsters sit at the big round table in the middle of the restaurant having a good time. The scene looks like it is straight out of the movie, *The Godfather.* Across the soft, low lite beige-colored room to the right of Sal and his friends, sitting fifty feet away at a round table against a wall, both dressed in suits and wearing glasses, are Flush and Mel. As they eat their plates of Lasagna with a clear view of Sal and his friends, Flush and Mel are waiting patiently for the right time to let King know when to make his move. King sits across the street from the restaurant, parked in an all-black S-Class Benz with Tone.

"Hey, I rented out the whole VIP section at your favorite strip club and then from there we will head over to Ty Warner's penthouse suite at the Four Seasons Hotel for the after party. So, it's gonna be a long night, my man. I hope you brought your Viagra with you," Sal said to his cousin.

"Get the fuck out of here! I ain't Fat Tony," the baby-faced Carmine replied.

"Hello," Sal said, answering his cell phone and getting up from the table.

"There's a hit out on you. Nando Sanchez ordered it and got a guy named King to take the contract," the man on the other end of the phone said.

"King?" Sal paused, trying to think if he had ever heard of him before. "Hold on, you talking about the mulignan, *(Italian for, Negro),* dope pusher from Queens?"

"Yes. I don't know when it's supposed to happen, but it's in motion."

"Who the fuck is this and how did you get my number?" Sal asked with a mystified look on his face. He didn't get an answer, the person on the other end hung up instead.

Walking back to the table with a smile on his face, Sal hears everyone in the restaurant joking and laughing and begins to get paranoid as he takes a seat next to his under boss, Dominick Sclafani.

"Hey, remember that mulignan that runs all that dope out there in Queens near our construction projects?" Sal whispered to Dom.

"Yeah, I remember him. Why? What happened?"

"I just got a call; apparently somebody put a hit out on me and he took the contract."

"What? Which family ordered the hit?" Dom asked as his old face turned red and he took off his glasses.

"Not a family; our little Spanish friend, Nando. Which really means Hector wants it done. A spic eating tacos in Mexico is gonna order a mulignan to take me out? Are they fucking crazy? I want Nando and King Dead immediately! You know who to call."

"I'm on it, Sal," Dom replied.

"Oh, yo Carmine…where you going? Your favorite song is on," Sal said, snapping his fingers and bopping his head as Carmine walked to the bathroom.

Sade's song, "Cherish the Day" plays through the speakers of the restaurant, blending in with the noise of people talking and laughing. Two beautiful Spanish women walk through the front door, catching Sal's attention and bringing a big smile to his face. His eyes widen as he stares at the two curvaceous women in tight dresses and high heels walking toward his section with the hostess.

I wouldn't want to gooooo...to heaven, Sal sang out load, bringing smiles to the faces of the two Spanish women. "Hey, how come you two gorgeous women walking in here without dates?" Sal asked them.

"I do have a date...with you!"

Boom!

Before Sal could reply, a bullet goes through his head causing his body to jerk back in his chair. The shot was followed by five more shots to his chest from the Glock 9mm handgun held by one of the Spanish women; causing him to fall backwards in his chair and to the floor. Fat Tony tried to rush the other Spanish woman and caught three bullets in the chest. He drops to the floor close to Sal. Pauly and little Nicky try to draw their guns, but are not quick enough as a bullet goes through Pauly's shoulder and two bullets go through little Nicky's stomach.

Running out the bathroom with his gun in hand after hearing gunshots and loud screaming, Carmine re-enters the dining room and sees tables flipped over and broken glass and chairs on the hardwood floor as his cousin, and his fellow mobsters are lying on the floor in puddles of blood. His adrenaline is pumping uncontrollably as he grips his gun and his eyes quickly scan the restaurant noticing people hiding under tables in fear; then he notices two women running toward the front door.

"It was them, Carmine," Pauly yelled out to him, pointing in the direction of the two women running toward the door.

Without any hesitation, Carmine raises his right arm and fires five shots at the two women, missing them and shattering the front glass door window.

"Marone! *(Italian for, damn it)* " Carmine said to himself as he hops over a chair and chases after them.

Making it out the restaurant un-touched, the two women hop into a black Audi that pulled up to the front of the restaurant as Carmine rushes out the front door and empties the rest of his clip at the bulletproof car as it speeds off.

"It's done," King said to Tone as they both watched the black Audi speed off and Carmine run back in the restaurant.

"What the fuck!" Carmine said, running back to the table. "Dom…you all right?" Carmine asked, watching as Dom got up.

"Yeah, I'm good. Is Sal breathing, Carmine? Please tell me he's breathing?"

"He's gone, Dom; he's cazzo andata, *(Italian for, he's fucking gone)* " Carmine replied looking at his cousin lying on his back with his eyes closed.

"Carmine, you have to get out of here before the cops come," Dom ordered him to do as he grabbed him by the shoulders and started walking with him to the back of the restaurant.

Residents and other store owners start to crowd around the front of Bella Luna. Some were taking pictures with their phones and others were staring in shock. Most thought the scene they witnessed reminded them of that unforgettable cold and snowy December night that took place in 1985 at Sparks Steakhouse in midtown Manhattan when the biggest mob boss in the country was gunned down.

Sitting in the living room of his house in Garden City, Long Island, Agent Bauer – along with his two young daughters and his wife – watches the new *Spider Man* movie. It's movie night at the Bauer's residence; as it is every Thursday.

"Why is he calling me right now? Pause the movie, Samantha. Hello," Agent Bauer said, answering his cell phone.

"Sam, can you hear me?" Agent Crebbs asked.

"Yeah, you're interrupting me from watching a movie with my family; it's movie night at the house. What's the problem?"

"Somebody just took out Big Sal at his restaurant Bella Luna."

"You're kidding me."

"Nope, it's on the news right now. Somebody just took out Sal Lombardo."

"All right, I'mma get dressed and head to the office; meet me there in forty-five minutes," Agent Bauer said, getting off of the couch and running to his bedroom.

Cups of Cognac sit on the round gambling table in the basement of King's house as he, Tone, Mel, Flush and Haze prepare a plan in case there's some blowback from the hit on Sal Lombardo. It's the biggest murder King has ordered in his life, and knowing that the Lombardo family has over fifteen hundred soldiers, King knew that there was the possibility of a very long war ahead that could claim a lot of lives.

"Everybody needs to be on the same page. Change up your routines; change up the pickup and drop off days. Everything needs to change. I want every spot we have to be swept for bugs, ASAP. Even y'all cars, cribs and whatever else y'all think needs to be swept. If the

Lombardos find out I was behind that hit, we will be at war for a very long time," King told everyone.

Boom! Boom! Boom!

The sound of a small hand banging on the basement door catches his attention. King gets up from his seat to see who it is.

"Nicole, it's two in the morning. What are you doing up? You're supposed to be sleeping," King looked at his daughter with inquiring eyes.

"I can't sleep and I see my uncles' cars in the driveway. I wanna hangout with y'all and play cards."

"Nicole, come here, I gotta tell you something," Mel said, waving her over.

Pushing her father out of the way and running into the room with a smile on her face, Nicole sees all of her uncles sitting at the table playing cards.

"You can chill for a little while, but you can't tell your mother," King said, closing the door.

"You know I'm not gonna say anything. Are y'all playing blackjack for money? That's my favorite game and I brought money with me," Nicole said, digging in her pajama pocket.

"What? How much money you got?" Flush asked, smiling at Nicole as she pulls out a knot of money.

Nicole pulls out a knot of money almost as big as the ones her uncles have in their pockets. Each of the men's eyes widen with a look of shock on their face. The first thing that runs through King's mind is that his daughter somehow got into his safe.

"Where did you get all that money from?" King asked.

"Uncle Tone...he always gives me money when he comes over and I saved it. Don't hate on me, daddy because I have more money than you right now."

"Yo, shrimp face...why you giving my daughter all that money? She has more than a couple hundred dollars in her pocket," King asked Tone in a curious tone waiting for him to reply.

The room suddenly got quiet and Nicole innocently stared at Tone, and then at her father as he shuffled the cards. Tone had a confused look on his face as he scratched his bald head wondering if King was actually mad at him or not; but his mind was eased and he could tell King was playing around once he saw a slight smile stretch across his face as he dealt out the cards.

"Hey," Tone responded, putting his hands in the air. "What you want me to do...say no? Have you tried to say no to that little girl?"

"Yeah, I know it's hard, but absolutely….I expect you to say no. She's gonna end up having more money than all of us at the rate she's going. That's a true hustler right there," King replied in a loud, joking tone and everyone started laughing.

*****

FBI Headquarters
26 Federal Plaza - 7th floor
Manhattan, New York

"A week and a half has gone by and we have no leads, at all, on the Sal Lombardo murder. The only thing we have to go on is that two Spanish women were involved, and our facial recognition program can't find out who they are. The shipment King's crew out in Jamaica was supposed to get was canceled because there's a leak in this office or within the agency itself. So, to put it kindly… we're fucked right now," Agent Bauer said to Agent Mackey.

"I know, Sam; but we're gonna have to come up with something because the agency is gonna give this case that we have been building on King to somebody else. Or they just gonna shut it down completely. It's been over a

150

year. We might just have to bend the rules. Nothing too serious, but I'm just saying…we're running out of options," Agent Mackey said with an air of frustration in his voice.

"Bend the rules? I've been doing this job for twenty years and I've never bent the rules. I'm not about to start now. We're just like the criminals we're chasing if we start doing that," Bauer responded.

"I guess. You know that motherfucker is opening up more businesses in Long Island City and on the Westside of Manhattan," Agent Mackey said, getting up and walking over to the window.

"Yeah, and they're all legit. No traces of drug money funding them. He's a smart man; I give him that. But karma is a bitch. You don't live a good life doing all the shit he has done. It catches up to you with either a bullet in the head or life in prison. It always happens. This is my last case and we're going to arrest him and I'mma put his ass away for life, before I retire."

Over the past twenty years, Agent Sam Bauer has put away a lot of big-time drug dealers, murders and Wall Street bankers. He's had a very successful career with the FBI, receiving awards and medals for his outstanding work that some agents can only dream of receiving one day. But this case is turning out to be the hardest case he's ever worked on.

"I hope we do, 'cause if we don't…this cock sucker is going to disappear with hundreds of millions dollars of blood money and never look back," Agent Mackey replied, staring out the window and down at the courtyard.

"We're going to get him; even if I gotta die trying, we'll get him," Agent Bauer assured him, pulling out a Marblo cigarette and walking over to the window. "Are you still bringing the wife and kids by for Thanksgiving?"

*****

The smell of turkey, stuffing, mac and cheese, rice, collard greens, lasagna, and a half a dozen different pies and desserts filled the air in King's house. The whole crew showed up for the first Thanksgiving dinner that he held at the new house. Everyone brought their girlfriend with them; even Tone, which surprised everyone because she was a Colombian woman in her mid-forties who was breathtaking. As all the men and Nicole sat in the living room watching the football game, all the women were in the kitchen cooking and talking. King was happy to see his whole crew still alive and enjoying themselves after the hit they pulled off two weeks ago.

Sitting in his recliner and sipping on a glass of Hennessy, a smile stretches across King's face as he watches Tone and Nicole argue over a blown call that caused the end of the first half of the game. King loved watching his babygirl be so intrigued with sports; unlike how he was when he was her age. Even though he played basketball when he was younger, he didn't care for it; it was just the thing to do. Shifting his eyes to Flush and Mel who were sitting on the sofa talking and laughing, makes King remember the first time he meet the both of them, and how loyal they had been to him ever since. Haze's loud voice catches King's attention as he watches him walk from the kitchen into the living room, already tipsy. King can't help but smirk and let out a slight laugh knowing that Haze could never hold his liquor; as big and menacing as Haze was, he was a light weight when it came to drinking.

"The turkeys are ready!" Kia yelled out as the women carried the platters of food one after another into the dining room.

"It's about time," Nicole said, running into the all-white dining room.

Standing up at the head of the fourteen-seat, custom-made, mahogany brown Versace dining table, King raises a glass of red wine in his hand.

"I would like to say a few words before we eat," King stated, looking at everyone at the table. "It's been a long and stressful road that we have been on for the past few years. It took each and every one of us working together in order to get where we are now and I'm very, very, thankful that we're all here to spend Thanksgiving together. Here's to good health and much more success…" he raises his glass higher. "I love all of y'all. Salute."

"We love you too, fam," S stated and everyone else shouted the same thing and joined in on the toast.

After everyone enjoyed the dinner, it was party time as oldies music played over the sound system in the living room and everyone began drinking and dancing.

"You think Tone flew that broad in from Colombia, acting like that's his girl? Haze asked King as they sat on the patio in the backyard smoking cigars.

"I have no idea; but with Tone…you never know," King replied as his eyes are fixated on the full moon in the dark sky. "How's everything looking out there? We're not losing any money; right?

"Nah, things are running smooth. We halfway done and payments have been in full and on time," Haze replied.

Exhaling the cigar smoke as he turns to his left and stares at the scar on Haze's face, King continues, "I heard

154

what you did to your cousin. I know that was family and it had to be hard for you to take him out like that; but it is what it is. He ran off with a quarter of a million dollars of work and we can't allow shit like that to happen; no matter who they are or who they are related to," King said to him.

"He was a scumbag. I could care less about that piece of shit," Haze replied in a strong tone.

Haze had found out that his cousin Kenny ran off to Richmond, Virginia with the four bricks of dope and setup shop down there with two of his people. Haze was able to get his house address and the name of the strip club he frequented. When he had the information, Haze took Fatal and another youngin named Red, down to Virginia with him and caught his cousin coming out of the strip club and followed him to his house. Once they got to the all-white, one-story house which was the last house on a dead-end street, Haze, Fatal and Red waited ten minutes and then bust through the front door. They caught Kenny and two of his workers that were there with him by surprise. Unable to get to their guns quick enough, Kenny and his two workers were forced into the kitchen by Fatal and Red at gunpoint and then tied up by Haze. Kenny thought he could buy his way out of the situation and told Haze he had a stash spot containing $150,000 located in the floor of his bedroom.

He thought that by giving Haze the money and the fact that they were cousins would be enough to spare his life; but Haze didn't care about the money. He let Fatal and Red keep it.

As Kenny and his two workers sat in chairs side by side tied up in the kitchen, they watched as Haze pulled out a power drill from a small gym bag he had carried in. Their eyes widened in fear and their begs for mercy echoed through the house as Haze turned on the power drill. After a half an hour of Haze, Fatal and Red taking turns torturing Kenny and his two workers by drilling holes in their legs, arms and feet Haze got bored and put a bullet in each of their heads, and then burned the house to the ground with their bodies in it.

"What's up with Mel and Flush? How are they doing out there?" King inquired.

"Same 'ol Mel and Flush…they are out there in the streets and taking care of business as usual. Why? Is there something I need to know about?

"Nah, I was just asking. You know them niggas don't tell me everything that's going on. They think I got so much shit on my plate that I don't need to be bothered with the little shit."

"I haven't had any problems with them. If I did, you would have known about it." Haze replied.

"What y'all niggas talking about?" S asked in a loud voice as he walked onto the patio and sat down next to King.

"We talking about your bitch ass!" King replied with a smirk on his face.

"Nigga, please! Yo, you know I have never asked you or anybody else in the crew this question…but why don't any of y'all have any kids? King is the only one with a kid out of all of y'all," S asked Haze.

Haze took a pull from his cigar and then looked at S like he was crazy. "I don't want any kids, my nigga; you know that. They are more trouble than they are worth and they end up tying your ass to their mothers for life. Ya'll can keep that life; it ain't for me. As far as them other niggas in there, you gonna have to ask them yourself."

"Man, y'all dudes are crazy, B. In this life we live, tomorrow's not promised. Y'all gotta start having kids to leave a part of you behind out here for when you gone. Think about Mac; he's gone and there's nobody to carry on his name," S replied.

"They don't need kids of their own; all of ya'll have a kid to take care of…Nicole," King stated and gracious

157

smiles spread across the faces of Haze and S as they sat back in their chairs and stared at the full moon while exhaling cigar smoke.

*****

The door opens and the overwhelming smell of Padron cigars hit the baby-faced Carmine Assante walking through the door of The Augusta Social Club located in Brownsville, Brooklyn. It's the hangout for the Lombardo crime family. The small storefront has been there since the seventies and has a very eerie feeling to it. The large window on the storefront is tinted so you can't see through from the street and the name, The Augusta, is painted in red paint in the middle of it. A small black wooden bench sits in front of the store, along with a three-foot, black stone statue of a bushel of roses next to it. The store is just fifty yards away from the elevated railway station that the number two train runs on.

Placing his beige Salvatore Ferragamo pea coat and his beige fedora on the coat rack along with removing his black Tom Ford sunglasses, the young Carmine takes a seat at the table. Across from him are Dominick Sclafani, aka, Dom, who's the new boss of the Lombardo family; and Joe

Bruno, the consigliore. Visibly irritated, Carmine lights up a cigarette and waits for Dom to tell him what's going on.

Even though he's sixty-five years old, Dom looked and moved around as if he were twenty years younger than what he really is. Life has been good to him and his kind and approachable appearance is very deceiving. The new boss of the Lombardo family is as ruthless of a mobster as you will ever come across; killing at the snap of a finger with no remorse. He's also very manipulative and demands and gets respect with ease.

"Listen, a guy we do business with named Nando ordered the hit on your cousin and some dope pusher from Queens named King carried it out. I have no idea why he ordered the hit; but we'll find out in due time. We just recently got some information on King; it took some time, but we got it. So he will be taken care of before the weekend is over," Dom assured Carmine.

"Good, because I was starting to wonder why it was taking so long," Carmine replied.

"Nando, on the other hand, is out of the country in a drug war with some other spic, so he's gonna be a little harder to get to right now. But believe me...his time is gonna come."

"Now what's going on with the three gambling spots Fat Tony ran? May God bless his soul; but did you come to a decision on that yet because I was next in line to take those over," Carmine asked.

"Yeah, I came to a decision. I'm giving it to Phil," Dom replied, watching Carmine's facial expression change immediately.

"Phil…your nephew?"

"Yeah…Phil, my nephew; he's older and he's not as much of a hothead as you are. You can't control your temper, Carmine; and you take too many chances. You act before thinking things through and I don't need that on my crew. Did you think I wasn't gonna find out about what you ordered your crew to do yesterday? I've been the boss for only two weeks now and I got captains doing shit behind my back."

"Behind your back? What? Are you fucking kidding me? I didn't do anything behind your back. We talked about it at that dinner that night. You and my cousin gave me the okay to do it. The two of you didn't have a problem with it; and by the way, here's your cut…seventy-five grand," Carmine said, dropping a white envelope on the table.

"Yeah, he was the boss; that's why I agreed with him. Now I'm the boss and you should have reminded me and I would have said no before you did it. I could care less about this seventy-five grand. You're lucky the Feds aren't on our asses 'cause of what you and your crew did."

"Well, it's too late now; it's been done," he gets up from his seat. "And you wrong for giving Phil those spots when they were supposed to be mine and everyone knows that. I'll remember it."

Hiding his anger, Carmine grabs his coat and fedora and walks calmly out the door and gets into his blue E-Class Mercedes Benz parked in front of the club.

Angelo knew the meeting went had gone badly when Carmine got in, slammed the door, and had a serious look on his face.

"That old fuck gave them to his nephew, Phil? Each spot clears no less than $25,000 a week in profit. Phil is gonna be making at least thirty to thirty-five grand a week extra on top of what he already makes with construction," an angered Carmine told his driver, Angelo.

"Fuck that old fuck and his pussy-ass nephew! I never liked him anyway," Angelo stated, driving off.

"We gotta stop by Moe's spot in Bayridge; I gotta make pick up. He owes me fifteen grand for the game the other night. The dumb fuck doesn't know shit about football. I tell you this also," he lights a cigarette. "That old fuck better not think I'm gonna be kicking up a piece of my cut from the online business I started," Carmine said.

"That old fuck is as greedy as they come; Carmine. You and I both know that."

Letting out a loud sigh as he looked out the window, Carmine replies, "He is greedy; but I hope he's not stupid!"

At only thirty years old, Carmine "Baby Face" Assante is considered by many as one of the most feared, up and coming mobsters of the 21st century. Light skinned with thick, black wavy hair and dark, closed-set eyes, Carmine stands 5'7" and a stocky two hundred and ten pounds. Besides his trigger-happy ways and his total disregard for the quality of life, it was his criminal intuition that helped him rise in the family ranks. He started out as a hit man for the Lombardo family at the age of seventeen and now he's a captain of his own crew, and the family's top earner. He got the nick name "Baby Face" from his cousin Sal because of his boyish looks and for the fact that he can't grow any facial hair.

He was born on November 8, in Brownsville, Brooklyn and raised by both of his parents: Joseph Assante and Karen Belotti Assante. His father, Joseph, was a captain on the rise in The Lombardo Family until he was gunned down during a robbery of a card game. Carmine was seventeen when his father was murdered and he vowed he would get revenge for his father's death no matter what; ignoring the orders of his cousin Sal, who had just become boss of the family at the time.

The young Carmine found out who one of the robbers was, and he saw him one day walking up the block toward him as he was standing in front of The Augusta Social Club. As the man approached, Carmine saw that he was smoking a cigarette and approached him with a cigarette in his mouth and asked the man for a light. As the man looked down and reached into his pocket for a light, he lifted his head and felt the gun placed in the middle of his forehead and looked into the eyes of Carmine as he pulled the trigger. In broad daylight, on a hot summer afternoon, in front of The Augusta Social Club, Carmine had just murdered the man that was involved in the murder of his father.

Sal and a few other mobsters rushed out of the front door of the club to see the dead man lying in front of them in a puddle of blood. Carmine ran down the block and out of sight.

Some captains were pissed that Carmine brought a lot of heat from the police on to the club and the family. That's not the way the family handled things and Sal started to hear the rumblings from the family about him not disciplining his cousin. The fact that Carmine's actions were making captains in the family a little upset as the weeks went on bothered Sal and a meeting took place to discuss the matter amongst Sal and the rest of the crew. Everyone came to a mutual agreement that Carmine would have to pay the family seventy-five thousand dollars by either coming up with the cash or work for the family doing whatever he was ordered to do until they felt the debt was paid off. But then Dom stood up at the meeting and spoke on Carmine's behalf and forever changed the minds and hearts of everyone at the meeting; including the way they looked at Carmine.

CHAPTER 8

"Whoever you want is dead and their wife and kids.

No mercy on any soul."

~S

Sunday, November 25, 4:00 p.m.

Queens, New York

It's the traditional football Sunday at Roses Coffee Shop and everyone is there watching the game; King, Haze, Mel, Tone, Flush, Hoffa and a couple of low-level soldiers in King's crew. As he does every Sunday, the young Fatal is out front barbecuing all types of food on the custom-made garbage can grill. Money is on the line for the Giants and Cowboy game which has come down to the last drive. King has twenty grand on his Giants against Hoffa's Cowboys. The score is 28-23 Cowboys, with one minute and thirty-five seconds left in the fourth quarter. The Giants have the ball on their own ten-yard line.

"Y'all not scoring on us and y'all have no timeouts left; this game is over, fam," Hoffa said with a big smile on his face with his arm around King's shoulder.

165

"Easy E ain't letting it go down like that; watch us drive right down the field," King stated, confident that his Giants would win.

"Man, fuck Eli. I guarantee you he will throw a pick, he always does when the pressures on," Hoffa said out loud.

"We'll see."

The smile on Hoffa's face quickly changed when Eli hit Cruz on a crossing route that went for sixty yards up the field to the Cowboys thirty-yard line on the third play of the drive, leaving forty seconds left on the clock. After getting sacked and losing slight yards, he dropped the ball down the field. Eli hit his tight end over the middle for twenty-four yards to the fourteen-yard line; leaving five seconds on the clock after spiking the ball.

"I told you, Easy E ain't playing with y'all. They can't stop us," a hyped-up King said as the ball is snapped.

"Get open, Cruz; get open. There it goes," King screamed out.

The place erupts as Eli throws a touchdown to Cruz in the back of the end zone to win the game. Hoffa takes a seat at a table pissed off; his Cowboys blew the game and he just lost twenty grand.

"I told you, fam never count us out; shit ain't over till it's over," King told Hoffa, taking a seat next to him. "Anyway, what's good with you? Is the money coming in proper like it should?"

"Yeah, shit popping upstate. I brought Gotti in as a partner so things are moving, fam," Hoffa replied.

"What's up with Gotti; he ain't fucking with me? I had everyone at my house Thursday for Thanksgiving except you and him. I knew you were out of town so that explains you, but he didn't even pick up his phone or call me back," King asked Hoffa, watching his reaction and if his droopy left eye started twitching which usually meant he was lying.

"I don't know, he didn't say anything to me about you, so I don't know; but you know how that nigga can be sometimes."

His left eye didn't twitch, King said to himself. "Yeah, I guess. Tell him to call me. I gotta talk to him about something anyway."

"I'll let 'em know. What's good with the spot you opening down the block? I see you bought the Chinese owners out," Hoffa asked.

"Yeah, I'm turning it into a lounge. The renovations should be done in a couple of weeks and it should be open for New Year's Eve."

King had just recently bought the two property's that were next door to each other which were a spacious Chinese restaurant and a dry cleaners a couple of months ago. Over the past year, King has been expanding his businesses by buying up properties in Long Island City and on the Westside of Manhattan on Columbus Avenue. He opened another Roses Coffee Shop on 90th Street and Columbus Avenue and an organic vegetable store on 88th Street and Columbus Avenue. He already has the Roses Coffee Shop in Long Island City, along with the Black Roses Lounge and an ice cream shop that would be opening soon. The stock market has also been good to King over the past year and a half; tripling the money he invested and making him millions.

"What's up, y'all finished?" King asked, answering his phone as Kia and Nicole are waiting for him to pick them up in the city.

"Yeah, we're walking to Bella's to get some ice cream. The movie was long as hell, but she had fun; she couldn't stop laughing," Kia replied.

"All right, I'm on my way. Just hang tight for a few."

Driving across the 59th Street Bridge and listing to the Patriot and Jets game on the radio, a smile arises on King's face as he stares at the picture of Kia and Nicole which hangs from his rearview mirror.

"Stay a little behind; don't get too close," Fish told Ant, the driver of the black Hummer. They, along with Dog, follow King's Range Rover off the 59th Street Bridge. Fish and his crew were paid $75,000 by the Lombardo family to kill King.

Driving up 3rd Avenue, the streets are damn near empty as they always are on a Sunday; usually everyone stays home except old people out for their weekly Sunday drive. Bella's is a world-renown ice cream shop on 71st Street and 3rd Avenue and it's Nicole's favorite place to go whenever they are in the city.

Holding a Heckler & Koch MP5 sub machine gun in his right hand and smoking a cigarette with the other, Fish watches as King pulls up and parks on 71st Street in front of Bella's.

"Pull up behind the blue van," Fish told Ant and he did as he was told. King's car was a few cars ahead of them. "Dog, are you ready?" Fish asked him.

"Yeah, I'm ready," Dog replied, holding a Glock 9mm in each hand.

Fish instructs Ant not get out of the car unless they're in trouble and they need help. They watch as King steps out of his car and stands in front of Bella's. His adrenaline pumping and heart racing, the eager Dog told Fish, "Let's do it now," as he opens the car door.

Rushing out the front door, ice cream in hand, screaming out, "Daddy, I got vanilla with sprinkles," Nicole brings a big smile to King's face as he picks her up and gives her a kiss on the cheek.

"Babe, I didn't get you anything, do you want something?" Kia asked him as she walks out the front door of Bella's.

"Nah, I'm good," King replied, putting Nicole down.

"Damn, he's got his family with him," Dog said to Fish, feeling a little hesitant about what they were about to do.

"I don't give a fuck about that nigga's family, it's lit," Fish replied as they creep on both sides of the blue van and then he locks eyes with Kia.

The look of shock and fear on Kia's face sent a chill through King's body as if someone or something was approaching him. He could see that her eyes were looking in the direction to the left side of his body and the fear in her eyes alerted him that something was up. *It's a hit,* he said to himself, grabbing Nicole's hand tightly and watching Kia's face turn back toward him as her mouth open up wide.

"King...to your left!" Kia screams out.

Rat, tat, tat, tat, tat, tat, tat.

Shots from Fish's MP5 riddle the mailbox in front of King and whiz by him and Nicole. *Fuck*! King said to himself as he pulls the Glock 9mm from his waist, turning and shielding Nicole with the left side of his body. He exchanges fire, forcing Fish to duck behind the trunk of a white car. Nicole is terrified, shaking and screaming as she's holding on to her father's leg with her eyes closed, twitching to every gunshot fired.

"King!" Kia screamed out at the top of her lungs as she crawled on the ground toward him.

Nicole hears the sound of her mother's voice and opens her watery, terrified eyes to the sight of her mother crawling toward her with blood covering her leg. "Mommy!" she screamed out as King moves toward Kia with Nicole stuck to his leg. He fires two shots at Dog who is trying to creep from behind the blue van and three more shots at Fish; hitting him in the neck. Dropping down to one knee, King pulls Kia toward him as he opens the back door of the car and Nicole jumps in.

Rat, tat, tat, tat, tat.

Shots from Ant's MP5 ricochet off the open back door as King closes it, and then opens the driver side door and Kia climbs in. King fires three shots at Ant and two of them hit him in the shoulder; causing him to drop his gun. The sound of gun shots to the left of him catches King's attention as he sees Dog shooting at the passenger side of his car, trying to shoot Kia and Nicole.

"Everything is gonna be fine, baby," Kia told Nicole as they duck down inside the car holding each other terrified, listening to bullets ricochet off the bulletproof car. King drops to the ground and fires four shots under the car. His bullets all hit and tear up Dog's ankles and feet; causing him to fall face first to the ground and eye to eye with King.

Boom!

King sends a hollow tip bullet that rips through Dog's head. The sounds of police sirens appear to get closer as people inside of Bella's and across the street are horrified at what they are witnessing unfold.

172

"Where's daddy at, mommy? Where's daddy?" Nicole asked as tears fall down her face, terrified that her father is dead.

"I'm right here, baby," King said, hopping in the car and then pulling off.

Looking into the rearview mirror, King sees the blood covering Kia's white pants as her face grimaces from the pain. Nicole wipes the tears from her eyes and tries to pull herself together.

"How bad is the wound, Kia?" King asked, speeding up York Avenue.

"It hurts, but I'll be fine. It went in and out; I think."

"Daddy, why were those men shooting at us? Why did they shoot mommy?" Nicole asked in a frightened tone as tears kept falling down her face.

"I don't know, baby girl. I don't know. But it's okay, everything is going to be all right, I promise you. We're going to get mommy to a doctor and everything is going to be fine," he assured her looking back and staring into her frightened eyes.

Pulling out his phone, King calls Rich, the owner of Bella's, and tells him to get rid of the camera footage of what happened in front of his shop, which the owner had already done by dumping a virus in his surveillance

173

system. Rich had a loyalty to King like most of the other business owners in the city, so he had no problem getting rid of anything that the police could later use against King.

Then King called his private doctor that he used for situations like this. He told him to meet him at Haze's loft off of Queens Plaza in fifteen minutes. After talking to the doctor, he then called Haze to let him know what had just gone down. Not panicking and displaying a calm demeanor as he pulled up to a red light in front of the ramp to the 59th street Bridge, King looked back at Kia and Nicole and winked at them and said, "Everything is going to be ok," even though the anger inside him was growing stronger and stronger, he didn't want his girls to worry.

*****

"Niggas just got at King, and Kia and Nicole were with him," Haze told the crew that was in the shop, after receiving a phone call from King. He wants us all at my spot, now!"

The anger and rage in the room mounted as everyone rushed out the shop and hopped in their cars; headed to Haze's loft.

"It had to be the Italians," Mel said to Haze as they sped down Vernon Boulevard.

"It was them or La Perla. So, either way...we at war," Haze replied as a million thoughts ran through his mind. Putting his family in danger had just taken his anger to a new level.

Hanging up his phone, the veins in Dom's neck and the right side of his forehead enlarge and everyone sitting in the Ozone Park apartment knew something had gone wrong with the hit on King.

"Idiot's! Fucking idiots! They let him get away. It's fucking amateur night out there. Find this mulignan I just talked to and take care of him; the other two are dead already. And call our brothers in Queens to take care of King," Dom told one of his top captains.

You should have used them from the get go like I said and we wouldn't be in this mess, Carmine said to himself, lighting a cigarette and staring at Dom pace around irritated.

Lying in Haze's bed with her leg wrapped and Nicole in her arms sleeping, Kia stares out the window at Roosevelt Island. The events of the day passed slowly through her mind. In all the years that King had been in the game, there never was a danger to her or her daughter.

Being that close to death scared her. She lowers her head and thanks God that Nicole wasn't hurt or killed. Thoughts of whether King will live or die from this moment on tears her up inside. She imagines that what she is feeling is what Asia must have felt when she lost Mac; the loss of the love of your life being taken from you in the blink of an eye. Rubbing Nicole's head and looking at her sleeping so peacefully makes Kia flash back to the image of Nicole holding on to her father's leg with her eyes closed and crying hysterically in the midst of gunfire. As she flashes back to the ice cream shop in her mind, Kia begins to tear up again as she lays back more fully against the pillow under her back.

King and his crew sat in Haze's living room racking their brains trying to figure out who was behind the hit.

"It could have been Luis Beltre; you said he wants to take shit over, and he's at war with the Rayon," Flush stated angered and craving revenge for what happened to King and his family.

"It's the Italian's. Luis Beltre would've used a bunch of wetbacks with M-16s to do the job; it would have been a lot sloppier, but they wouldn't have given up and me, Kia and Nicole would be dead right now. It's them other motherfucker's," King replied.

"Aight," Haze hung up his phone. "Tone got rid of the car and since the surveillance cameras in the store were taken care of, we should be good on the police front," he said before putting his hand on King's shoulder.

Staring at everyone's face and reading their body language, King starts to second guess whether someone sitting in the living room with him might have been the one to set him up. He couldn't help but wonder if someone on his team wanted him dead.

Who would have the balls to set me up? he thinks to himself, leaning back on the couch.

"Your cousin just pulled up," Mel told King as he went downstairs to let S in.

Everyone in the living room can hear the loud sound of S's heavy feet rushing up the stairs. "Fam, thank God y'all are all right," S said, walking through the door and hugging King as a tear falls down his cheek.

"Yeah…we're good. The girls are in the room; asleep. Kia got hit in the leg, but she's good though. It went in one side and out the other. Doc patched her up and she's just takin' it easy."

"Who the fuck was it?" S asked.

"I'm pretty sure it was the Lombardo Family. We were the ones that took out Big Sal Lombardo, so this is probably payback for that," King answered, rubbing at the tension headache forming above his eyes.

"That was you that did that hit? Fam, you're crazy," S said, staring at the anger in his cousin's eyes and wondering why he's just now finding out about it. "But, it is what it is. Whoever you want dead is dead; and so are and their wife and kids. No mercy on any soul, my nigga; straight up."

The sound of S's distinctive voice wakes Nicole up. Noticing that her mother is sleeping, she eases her way out of her mother's arms and sneaks out of the bed.

The room suddenly got quite and smiles appear on everyone's face as they watch Nicole walk into the living room wiping her eyes and walking over to S. He picks her up and puts her on his lap. King stops himself from tearing up as he looks at his babygirl lay in his cousin's arms. Just the thought of losing her or Kia would crush him.

"Nicole, what are you doing up?" S asked her as he stared at the tired look on her face.

"I heard your voice and I couldn't go back to sleep," she replied as she rested her head on his shoulder.

"I'm sorry I woke you up. I should have kept my voice down," he replied and then kissed her on the forehead.

The room remained silent as everyone did their best to hold back from shedding tears as they stared at Nicole falling asleep again as her head rested comfortably on S's shoulder. But Tone couldn't keep his composer and got up from the couch with tears falling down his face; walking pass King and toward the bathroom.

"I'll put her back in the bedroom," S whispered to King as he got up from the chair and walked toward the back of the house.

*****

FBI Headquarters
26 Federal Plaza - 7th floor
Manhattan, New York

The sound of the copy machine and fingers hitting a keyboard outside of the conference room pisses Agent Bauer off. He looks at the two bulletin boards in front of him; one board has pictures of King and his crew on it, the other has pictures of the whole Rayon Cartel on it. Dozens upon dozens of files are spread across the conference table which contains nothing he can use against King. Feeling desperate, the conversation he had with Agent Mackey about bending the rules starts to play back in his mind, but its cut short when he hears someone knocking on the door.

Agent Morris knocks on the door of the conference room; he has a concerned look on his face. He is holding a set of folders with *Classified* stamped across them in bold red letters. A look of disappointment appears on Bauer's face. Given the look on Morris' face, Bauer figures that the visit can't be anything but more bad news. He waves Agent Morris into the room and tells him to close the door.

"We have a real problem on our hands, Sam," Agent Morris said, dropping the folders on the table and sitting down. "I came across these files after doing some work on the Sal Lambardo murder. They were hidden under a secret operation name and everyone in these files was listed under fake names, social security numbers and fingerprints. It's unbelievable, Sam," Agent Morris said, handing him the folders.

"They're all informants? Every single one of them is an informant?" Agent Bauer is shocked and mystified, looking at the files. Two of them stand out to him, causing him to lean back in his chair and think for a second. "These two are high-profile and were killed within the last year and a half. They both were giving us information on the Rayon

Cartel from what I'm reading here. You gotta be kidding me."

"I'm guessing...matter of fact, I'm certain...the Rayon Cartel found out they were informants and had them killed. None of those murders were over a beef they had with anyone; their covers were blown. There's a fucking leak in the agency," Agent Morris said.

"You're right, and the only way they could get it done was by getting someone as powerful as that man right there," Agent Bauer points to King's picture on the board. *You slick son of a bitch, you out here painting the city red; aren't you. Now it all makes sense.* "Shit...but we still have to find a way to link all of this together, and how the fuck are we gonna do that?"

"I have no idea. But it's late and I'm about to head home. You can figure it out and let me know something in the morning," Agent Morris replied.

Someway, somehow...I'm gonna nail your ass, Agent Bauer said to himself about King. He looks through the files, shaking his head at the faces he sees inside. He is baffled that they are informants working with the FBI until he sees a face that looks familiar to him.

"Well, say it ain't so," he lets out a slight laugh. "This guy right here..." he shows Agent Morris the file, "…is gonna help us bring down everybody on both of those boards. Motherfuckin' jackpot, baby!"

The lyrics from the song, "I Still Haven't Found What I'm Looking For" come through the sound system in the living room of King's house. He and Nicole are singing and dancing, having a good time as Kia smiles, laughs and records the both of them on her phone.

"Come on, mommy…you gotta dance with daddy before he leaves because I need a break. I'm getting dizzy," Nicole said, walking over to her mother.

"Okay, I'll dance with daddy. Hann, record us," Kia said as she gets up and King pulls her close to him. They dance slowly, bringing a smile to Nicole's face. Her parents have always been affectionate around her and it's the only life she knows.

It's been a few days since the shooting at Bella's ice cream shop and Nicole hasn't brought it back up to her parents at all. At first, they worried if she would be traumatized about the shooting, but she seemed to be handling it well. Nicole believed the words her father told her when he promised her that everything was going to be all right, and she is just happy to see her parents smiling, dancing and having a good time like they always do.

Light rain falls on the streets of Bay Ridge, Brooklyn as Pete and Richie, who are captains in the Lombardo family, are waiting on Carmine to show up to settle a beef between their crews over a truckload of stolen Apple Mac laptops.

Didn't I tell this fucking guy to meet us on 63rd Street and 11th Avenue at three o'clock? Richie thinks to himself, growing impatient.

"Where the fuck is this kid? He's the one that called for this little sit down," Joe Bruno, the consigliore of the Lombardo family, asked as he walks out the front door of the Italian Deli. "Call him and find out what's going on," he told Richie.

"I did; his phone goes straight to voicemail," Richie replied, shaking his head.

"All right, let's go inside and wait a little while longer. Hopefully this kid will show up soon; I've got other shit to do," Joe said, walking back inside.

"You think something happened to Carmine? Because that other thing is in motion as we speak," Pete asked Joe as they walk to the back of the deli to the seating area outside.

Taking a deep breath and scratching his forehead, Joe starts to think something might have happened to

Carmine. "Make a few calls to his crew; find out if they saw him today or last night."

Sitting across the street from Roses Coffee Shop in a black Tahoe are Agents Donaldson and Crebbs. They watch as Haze, Tone, Mel and Flush arrive at Roses and walk in. "All these businesses off of drug money and blood. How much money do you think he makes?" Agent Crebbs asked Donaldson in regards to King.

"Who really knows? He and his crew probably made a hundred million within the past year; probably more. It always comes to an end; and speaking of the devil himself...there he goes...Mr. King," Agent Donaldson said as they watched King get out of his Hummer, and walk into the shop.

"Hey, watch how you park; you almost hit me," a short, Italian man said to the driver of the white van with the word's, *Vito's Imported Italian Meats* on both sides of it. The two men inside of the van hop out and unload two small crates of imported salami and prosciutto and walk into the Italian deli. Walking into the empty deli, they are greeted rudely by the owner; a short middle-aged Italian man who told them he didn't have any shipments scheduled for today.

"We were scheduled to deliver it two days from now, but our company is in a battle with the State over some licensing issues, so we gonna be shut down for a week or two," the tall and husky Spanish man wearing smoke gray shades told the owner.

"I thought that was Carmine he was talking to, but it's just delivery men," Pete said, sitting back down at the table outside.

"Put the crates there and open them up. What company are you from?" the owner asked, walking around the counter to get his schedule planner.

"We're from Vito's Imported Italian Meats," S said, opening the crate and pulling out a MP5 with a silencer. He held it behind his back as the owner comes from behind the counter looking in his schedule planner.

"I don't see your company in here for no deliveries," the owner says as he curiously flips through the pages in front of him.

The back end of Macho's gun knocks the owner out cold and then he drags him behind the counter. Creeping to the back of the deli, S can hear Joe and company talking as he sees the heavyset old man with glasses sitting with his back to the wall and two people in front of him. Cigar in his right hand and laughing at a joke Richie is telling, Joe looks into the shadow of the doorway. Before his facial expression could change...

Boom!

Pete and Richie watch as a hole appears in Joe's forehead and his brains fly backward, saturating the wall behind him. Richie tries to react as Pete is stuck in shock and both of them are riddled with bullets without even getting a glimpse of the gunman. Standing over Pete and Richie, Macho fills their bodies with more bullets as S walks over to Joe and does the same.

Waiting for a text and sitting amongst everybody in the coffee shop watching MSNBC, King is on his second cup of coffee and getting anxious; thinking something went wrong with his cousin.

"Those motherfuckers out there are crazy; they be having the Federal police and the military shook," Tone said about what they are watching on TV. It's the drug war between the Rayon and La Perla Cartels taking place in Mexico. Three high-ranking Federal police officers who were being paid off by the Rayon cartel for their help were shot and killed outside of their police station by two members of the La Perla cartel who walked up on the officers and opened fire on them with Colt M16-A1 automatic rifles.

"Honestly, that's the only way for them to get rich out there. They don't have any options out there in Mexico or anywhere in South America, at that. All they know is the drug trade from a child until the day they die. That's the way of life there; more so than what we do out here. Or, they learn how to swing a baseball bat or they risk their lives trying to sneak into this country. There's not a million and one ways to get rich like it is in America. The news coverage we're watching right now happens every day out there. The cartels don't hesitate and have no problem killing government officials, judges, lawyers, police and etc. Niggas like us get rich because of the blood they shed over there; And don't forget our crooked ass government that helps them bring the drugs over here get rich too," King said as he looks at a text message coming in on his phone.

That movie you told me about was good, the text read, which is code for: the job got done.

"It's done. He just hit me," King told everyone, feeling a sigh of relief like everyone else in the shop that his cousin came through. Taking a deep breath and leaning back in his chair scanning everybody's body language, King still has the feeling that someone in the room is moving against him.

"All right…y'all gotta go meet up with our friend in the Bronx and see what's going on with that problem we got out there that I told you about yesterday," King told Mel and Tone. "See if y'all can talk some sense into them Haitians; we're starting to lose money. I don't wanna be laying niggas down up there. We got enough problems already."

"We'll handle it, fam," Tone said as he and Mel give King a hug and pound and walked out the door.

CHAPTER 9

"Oh, word...family hug and y'all don't call me."

~Nicole

To King and his crew and the FBI agents staked out across the street, it felt like they were filming a scene on the set of an action movie. The foundation of the shop shook, causing the storefront window to shatter; sending glass flying everywhere. The impact of the blast knocked everyone out of their chairs and set car alarms off up and down the block. Dusting glass off of them and rising to their feet, everyone watches as the black Benz Tone and Mel got in, becomes engulfed in flames. Lost for words, King rushes out the shop to see if either of them are still alive; knowing in his heart that they are both dead. The thick gray smoke rises in the air as the rain falls and the loud sound of fire trucks approach the vicinity.

"This is unbelievable," Agent Crebbs said, shaking his head; still in shock from what he and his partner just witnessed.

"I gotta call Sam," Agent Donaldson said, pulling out his phone. "Come on...pick up the damn phone. Sam, can you hear me?"

"Yeah, what's going on," Agent Bauer replied.

"Tone and Mel were just blown up in a car bomb in front of Roses coffee shop. Crebbs and I saw it all go down."

"I knew it; they are at war with the Italians. Fifteen minutes ago, a bulletin came up reporting that Joe Bruno and two other Lombardo family members were gunned down in Bayridge Brooklyn. Have you left the shop already?" Agent Bauer asked.

"No, we're still here. The fire trucks just arrived; along with the police."

"All right, head back to the office now."

Tears fall down Flush's face as he becomes overwhelmed with emotion. He sits down on the ground in front of the shop, watching the fireman put out the flames of what used to be Tone's car.

"King, somebody was watching us. That shit was detonated; that wasn't a timer," Haze stated as they both look around the block at cars, people standing around, and the apartment windows on the block.

"Send our surveillance footage to your computer and then put a virus in the system here before the police get to it. And call our friend to see if he can hack into the systems of all the stores in that area to help us out," King instructed him.

Standing, shaking his head, and staring at the incinerated car in disbelief, King's heart jumped as he pulls out his phone and calls Kia. Picking up after the second ring, he was able to tell Kia to stay at the birthday party her and Nicole are at until he can get there to pick them up. As he hangs up, two police officers approach him.

"My man, are you the owner of this store?" an officer asks King.

"Yes, I am."

"My partner and I have a few questions we need to ask you."

After answering the cop's questions, King called Fatal and had him and a few of his youngins come and clean up the shop as he, Haze and Flush rush to the birthday party in Forrest Hills to pick up Kia and Nicole.

Terrified after hearing what happened to Mel and Tone, Kia demanded King to take her and Nicole to their house in Pennsylvania, until it was safe for them to comeback. Standing in the doorway of his bedroom watching as Kia packed her and Nicole's clothes in suitcases breaks his heart. As tears pour down her face and feeling sacred and nervous, Kia can't help but think she

191

might never see King again after he drops them off in Pennsylvania.

"Mac, Tone, Mel...and they tried to kill me, you and Nicole; whoever it is, is not gonna stop until they kill you, King. Why don't you see that?" she pleaded to him.

Walking up behind her, grabbing and turning her around, King wipes the tears from her face and hugs her tightly. "Look at me. I'm gonna take care of everything. I promise. Nobody's gonna stop me from being there for y'all; and I mean nobody! I give you my word."

Closing her eyes and resting her head on his chest, Kia takes a deep breath. She felt at ease after hearing exactly what she wanted to hear – a promise that he would never leave them. Opening her eyes, she sees Nicole standing in the doorway with a shocked look on her face.

"Oh, word…a family hug and y'all didn't call me," Nicole said as she runs in the room and hugs both of her parents. "We gonna have fun up there. We gonna mess with the deer, BBQ, and make marshmallows in the fireplace."

What the fuck is taking them so long? Haze said to himself as he and Flush are sitting in a Hummer in King's driveway along with Fatal and one of his soldiers sitting behind them in another Hummer.

"Here they go," Flush said as King and the girls come out the front door with S, putting the bags into King's Hummer.

"I'll be back tomorrow afternoon. So, I'll call you when we get there and when I'm on my way back tomorrow. And make sure your niggas don't break anything in there," King tells his cousin and then gives him a hug.

"I got you, fam. We're gonna take care of your house, don't worry."

"Andiamo! (*Italian for, Let's go*)" King yelled in the air to the other Hummers as he hopped into his.

"You gotta put my girl, Ellie's album on while we drive up there. I need to hear my song, "Explosions," Nicole said to her father.

The three black Hummers drive down the mixed stone driveway to the towering black steel gates at the entrance and off of the estate.

The inside of the Augusta Social Club is silent as Carmine and the other captains of the Lombardo family are awaiting Dom's arrival. A couple of the captains are starting to think that Carmine might have had something to do with the hit on Joe, Pete and Richie. It was a sit down Carmine called for, and yet he never showed up. The men

193

voiced their concern to Dom, and he wanted a sit down with everybody.

Walking through the door with his bodyguard, Dom asked with a disgusted look on his face, "Whose Porsche Panamera is that outside?"

"It's Baby Face's car," one of the captains said, referring to Carmine.

"Wow. That's what...over $70,000? What...did you hit it big in Atlantic City yesterday? Because you called for something and then you didn't show up," Dom said to Carmine as he sits down. "Maybe if you would have canceled the meeting, three of my men would still be alive. So, tell me straight up, Carmine...is there blood on your hands?" the look in Dom's eyes was more than accusing, it was deadly.

Taking a pull from his Newport and leaning forward in his seat, the words Carmine were about to say were gonna forever change the landscape of the Lombardo crime family and La Cosa Nostra in America.

"The only blood that's on my hands is the motherfucker that was involved in my father's murder; the one's I was ordered to do and the orders I gave. What happened yesterday was not on my hands," he pulls out his cell phone. "This right here is the text I sent Richie at ten in the morning yesterday. I told him I couldn't show up, so cancel it. But the piece of shit snake never said anything, I guess. And you know what…" he stands up and does a Hail Mary. "God bless, Pete and Joe souls; but fuck Richie and the twat that birthed him. The blood is on his hands and yours. You sent amateurs at a motherfucker that's more ruthless than you and now the score is four to two; they're winning. My cousin is turning in his grave."

"Carmine, calm down. You're way out of line right now; calm down," Carlo Licata, a high ranking captain in the family, told him.

"So, you think 'cause Richie might have been a snake, that you can raise your voice and disrespect me in such a way like that? I should let you walk out that front door, instead of your body being carried out in separate garbage bags," Dom replied as he leaned back in his chair. "The balls on this guy. You're an ungrateful fuck with a big mouth. The only reason you're a captain is because of me. Your cousin didn't wanna make you one, but I talked him into it. The only reason your ass wasn't disciplined for what you did years ago, was because of me. I'm the reason you sitting here today. You hear me! So don't tell me that Sal is turning in his grave. I'm the boss of this family. You're not just gonna run around here and do what you want and run your mouth. You and your crew of psychopaths are out of control right now. This ain't the nineteen-thirties; grow the fuck up!" Dom stated in an angered tone.

You could hear a pin drop in the Augusta after Dom spoke. Everyone watched as he and Carmine sat across from each other staring at one another. The smirk on Carmine's face was priceless as he put out his cigarette and unloosened his tie.

"You're the reason I'm sitting here? Sorry, but for some reason I didn't get that memo. The real reason I'm sitting here is because I make this family money and my reputation keeps certain people alive. In this thing of ours, the other families don't move on us 'cause of me. You know that. Right now, we're at war with a different animal; a mulignan that La Cosa Nostra ain't seen since the days of Bumpy Johnson. So where are we now?" Carmine said, raising his voice. "Playing tit for tat? It's been weeks...weeks! And we're here today 'cause all of a sudden, my loyalty has come into question," he gets up and puts on his brown pea coat. "So, you know what? I'll do the motherfucker myself; it will save you the trouble. Worry about business; something y'all are good at," Carmine said as he and Angelo walk out of the Augusta.

"He has to go," Frankie DeMato, the underboss, whispered into Dom's ear.

Lighting a cigarette and watching the train ride past on the overhead railway, Carmine knows what has to be done; even if it's against the rules and the Commission wouldn't approve it.

"You know what you just started?" Angelo asked Carmine, staring him in the eyes. "You are one crazy motherfucker, but I'm with you all the way."

"Fino alla morte, *(Italina for, Until death)*" Carmine said as they got in the car and drove off.

A smile stretches across Hector Santiago's wrinkled face as he watches his number one racing horse, Don Pepe, run toward him as he approaches the wooden fence. Hector Santiago, nick named The Grim Reaper, started the Rayon Cartel seventeen years ago and grew them into the largest and richest Cartel in all of Mexico. Ruthless, psychopathic, elusive, cunning, and sophisticated all describe Hector. His net worth is listed at 1.1 billion dollars, which earned him a spot in *Forbes* magazine as one of the richest men in the world.

"That was our friend from Queens and he has a problem on his hands. I don't know how the Lombardos found out we ordered the hit on Sal and that King took the contract. He's been at war with them and it's gotten real bad," Nando told Hector as he stands next to him. Hector watches Don Pepe and four of his other horses being trained on the two-acre horse ranch on his hideout estate in the mountains of Sinaloa.

It's been over a month now and the war with La Perla is still going on. Three hundred and thirteen people combined on both sides have lost their lives so far in the drug war. Hector thinks because his cartel is too large for the La Perla that Luis Beltre will be killed or he would eventually surrender and give up control of his drug operation in Puerto Rico. The thing Hector doesn't know is that Luis vowed he would not stop the war and has been offering ten million dollars to anyone who would give him the location of Hector, and three million dollars for the locations of his top commanders. The Presidents of Mexico and Puerto Rico have even reached out to the U.S. government for help on the matter before it starts to spill over into the U.S.

"The shipment we had planned for King, we have to delay it a week. I told him I don't know how you're gonna feel about it," Nando said to Hector.

"What? Is he...crazy? I know he's been loyal; but that's twenty million dollars of dope we need out of this country before the military or the La Perla gets to it. Either he takes it or finds someone else who will. We don't have time for any delays."

"Not a problem. I'll let him know tonight. Now I've been told that Luis is somewhere in Fajardo and he's being protected by the military; but that's not the bad part. The bad part is he's offering our own people out here; ten million dollars for your location and three million for mine and a few others. And, he also has two body doubles moving around Puerto Rico and that's a problem."

"Smart man, but we're smarter and stronger. I want that distribution port, and he and his brothers are standing in the way of that. You hear me?" Hector replied in a dark tone.

"I understand," Nando replied.

"Good. Now how many La Perla members you have over there in the shed?"

"Eight young boys; none of them look a day over twenty-one," Nando replied, watching Hector light up a cigar.

Exhaling the cigar smoke as a devilish grin appears on his face, Hector loved these moments as he and Nando walked over to the shed and Hector had his men decapitate the heads of the eight teenage La Perla members as he watched. Then he had his men drive into Hermosillo, the capital of Sonora, Mexico and hang the decapitated heads from Federal Highway 15, for everyone to see.

Sitting on a bench on Roosevelt Island, King waits on Haze as he watches a helicopter flies over the Manhattan skyline. The slamming of a car door quickly catches his attention as he turns around and sees Haze walking through the grass toward him.

"What's the word today?" Haze asked, taking a seat next to him.

"I talked to Nando this morning and told him to delay the shipment one week so we can find new storages. I don't know if the Italians got the drop on the ones we have already. I can't take that chance with all that product," King told him.

"Honestly, he's not gonna give a fuck. You know that. They are at war right now and he has to move all that before something happens out there. We have no choice, we gotta take it or he's gonna find someone else who will."

Scratching his head and leaning back on the bench, King stares at the United Nations building. He asks himself whether he should fall back and let Haze run everything.

"I'm going to do one more year of this and then you're gonna take over for me. You'll be in charge of everything, but I'll still be in the background."

"What?" Haze said, looking at King's face and noticing that he's serious. "You're sure you wanna do that? I got no problem with taking over; but I know how you are, my nigga. What the fuck are you gonna do? You've been in this game longer than we both can remember. What will you do if you're not doing this?"

"Run my other businesses; teach Nicole sports. You know...every day regular shit that normal people do."

Haze looked at King like he had lost his mind. He shook his head, but he knew King was not going to hand everything over just like that. The streets were too deep in his blood for him to walk away so quickly.

"You know...it's crazy that we never found out who had Mac killed though. It's been over a year and nobody knows shit."

"Of course we're not gonna find out who ordered it. They know I'mma kill their whole family if I ever find out. So, whoever did it is never gonna let that it get out that they are behind it. Shit, Nando can't even find out who ordered it and he has connections inside the FBI. So, it is what it is for now. But if I ever found out who did it..." he smiles at Haze and gets up from the bench.

Meanwhile 1,788 miles from New York, its eight-five degrees and the sun is shining brightly; bouncing off of the clear blue water of the North Atlantic Ocean.

"I'm telling you, he's gonna give up. We're winning and what we have planned tomorrow will bring this war to an end," Luis said to his brothers, Juan and Jose, as they sit in Luis's backyard of his ocean-front estate in Fajardo, Puerto Rico. The beautiful estate is guarded by thirty ex-military soldiers in station posts, the roof tops, as well as roaming the grounds around the clock.

"Have you contacted King yet to let him know about the change that's coming?" the younger brother Jose asked Luis.

"No. Not yet. God damn these fuckin' coquis are running wild in this part of the yard, Jesus Christ!" Luis complained, stomping on one with his sneaker. "Like I was saying...I'll do it soon; along with everyone else Hector was selling to in America. You know Nando still hasn't given me an answer yet. So, I guess he's standing by Hector and is willing to go down with the ship."

Luis made Nando an offer of overlooking the operation in America while his brothers ran everything in

Puerto Rico and Mexico. But Nando hasn't given Luis an answer yet because Hector has surveillance 24/7 on Nando and all of his phones tapped and the houses and cars bugged. Hector has been through too many drug wars during his reign in Mexico to trust anyone enough that they could possibly bring forth his demise.

"I think Nando will come around afterwards. He's probably just waiting because I don't think he's that stupid to turn down that much money. It's double what Hector pays him. But if he is, "Que Te Quemes en El infierno, (*Spanish for, He could burn in hell*)" Juan said, holding his coffee cup in the air.

We'll see, Luis said to himself, staring out into the ocean and taking a pull from his Cuban cigar. "I forgot to tell y'all my boy, Carlos, is gonna be the starting short-stop for his varsity team this spring. He is going to the majors, I tell you. He's that good. Jose, every game I go to…he hits a homerun; no lie. The two of you need to stop being lazy and come to Queens this spring and watch him play. He would love to see his uncles."

CHAPTER 10

"May God be with those in the way."

~Luis Beltre

FBI Headquarters

26 Federal Plaza - 7th floor

Manhattan, New York

Standing in the front of a packed conference room inside the FBI field office, Agent Bauer explains to the other agents in detail his plan on how they might be able to bring down King, along with the Rayon Cartel. Believing in his plan and having convinced the other agents to believe in it also, everyone gets on board with him and are ready to put his plan into motion. "Like I just said a little while ago, he is the key to the plan being successful," Agent Bauer said.

"You're sure he's just gonna go along with it, especially coming out of nowhere?" Agent Donaldson asked Agent Bauer.

"He has no choice; trust me. So let's get Mr....what the fuck is he doing here?" Agent Bauer said, looking at one of the heads of the FBI – Justin Abbott – walking into the office.

"Excuse me everybody...Agent Bauer, we need to have a talk. Alone!" Agent Abbott said in a stern voice and a serious look on his face.

As the rest of the agents walk out of the room, Agent Bauer knew that heads of the agency must have found out about Agent Morris coming across the classified files.

"I know bringing down King and his crew and hopefully the Rayon Cartel, is a top priority to the agency, but Agent Morris is going to be fired for what he did. And you need to stop any plan you have of using anyone in those files to take down King. They are government informants and they're protected for a reason; that's why it's classified information. As soon as he brought you those files, you should have given them back immediately. Now please tell me you weren't stupid enough to let all the agents that were just in here know who the informants are," Agent Abbott asked.

Staring at Agent Abbott like he had two heads, Agent Bauer takes a sip of water to calm himself down before going haywire. "First of all, Agent Morris should have only been suspended...not fired; he's not a rouge agent and you know it. The person whose job it is to keep those files classified should be fired; they are the one who wasn't doing a good enough job. Second, I've been here twenty years and I've been dedicated and helped this agency immensely. The agency had two of its biggest informants murdered within the past year and a half and does nothing about it. It also has other informants still dealing drugs and committing murders right under our nose. We look like fucking clowns out here. I'm trying to bring down King; he's the motherfucker that killed our informants and a bunch of other people on the side. He and his crew are at war right now with the Lombardo family. King is ordering hits in public places and the Lombardos are blowing up cars. Not to mention, he's made over a hundred million dollars over the past year working with the Rayon Cartel that's supplying him with the dope he's flooding New York with. But now y'all wanna get mad and do your jobs when other people find out the truth."

"You got any proof that King had those informants killed?" Agent Abbott asked, knowing what the answer was gonna be.

"Not, yet…but you just don't go to war with the mob for no reason. There's a leak in the agency that's giving up the names of the informants."

"Agent Morris stole files that were classified and he shared them with another agent. That's the truth and that's the main subject. We know those informants were murdered because their cover was blown. That's the price of being an informant. They knew that. So, I don't want you contacting anyone in those files. You wanna bring King down, do it without those informants. If I hear that you contacted any one of them, I'll have you brought up on charges. Do I make myself clear?"

"Yes. I hear you loud and clear," Agent Bauer responded, knowing damn well he's still going to go ahead with his plan; he has a lot of loyal friends within the agency that will go to hell and back for him. Agent Abbott knows it because he's one of them. That's why he didn't discipline him.

"All right, good...I'm glad you understand," Abbott said, getting up and heading toward the door. "Oh, yeah... and that board you got there with Hector and the rest of the Rayon Cartel on it."

"What about it?"

"Get rid of all the pictures. You need to start a whole new one with the La Perla Cartel. Luis Beltre is the new poster boy for the drug lords."

So, the La Perlas are gonna win the war. Which means King is about to have a new connect. What the fuck? If it ain't one thing it's another, Agent Bauer said to himself, opening up the window and sitting on the ledge. As he exhales the smoke from his Marblo cigarette, he stares at the sun going down in New York. Later on in the night, a change would take place in Mexico.

Hermosillo, New Mexico

Night falls on Hermosillo, the capital of Sonora, Mexico. The majority of the Rayon Cartel's storage facilities that house their drugs are located in this city. The city has 2.7 million residents and has been ran by the Cartel for fifteen years now, and even though the Governor of Sonora and the President of Mexico say they are going to do whatever it takes to bring down the Cartel; nothing has changed. If anything, matters have only gotten worse.

The streets up and down Kino Boulevard are packed with residents and tourists enjoying the beautiful night clubs, restaurants and bars. The majority of them are owned by Hector Santiago, the leader of the Rayon Cartel. The most popular night club in the city and owned by Hector is, El Selva. Hector and members of his cartel are there all the time; partying into the early hours of the morning.

On this night, Hector and forty members of his cartel are having a dinner party at his restaurant, Toloache. Trays of Pollo Toloache, Carne Asada, Tumbada and Langosta sit on the long buffet table for everybody to enjoy; along with dozens upon dozens of bottles of Casa Sauza XA Tequila. Songs by Beto Quintanilla play over the sound system as people dance and have a good time in the lounge area.

Dressed in a white silk shirt, beige dress pants and brown hard bottoms and entertaining a group of rich investors, is Hector. He is sharing his ideas of new businesses that can be started in Cabo and Cancun to make more money off of the tourists. He's always finding other ways to make extra money outside of his drug business which just adds to the hate the rival Mexican Cartels have for him.

"Nando, Felix…" Hector said, waving them over to him. He introduces them to the investors he's talking to.

After the dinner party, Hector and his forty-man entourage head to his club, El Selva, to enjoy the rest of the night drinking and partying. Dumping the ashes of his Cuban cigar out of the Hummer's passenger side window and staring at the empty streets, Luis Beltre inhales the musty smell of Sonora, Mexico. He and his forty-car convoy of bombproof black Hummers filled with one hundred members of his army who are all ex-military drive down Santa Anna Boulevard at four o'clock in the morning. Luis and his army are in town to take down the Rayon Cartel before the morning news airs.

His friendship with the leader of a rival cartel of the Rayon's helped him and his army sneak into Mexico undetected, and they supplied them with everything they would need to carry out the attack he has planned. Every member of his cartel is dressed in an all-black, bulletproof uniform and hat; they are also armed with a M4 Carbine machine gun, a Glock 19 and night vision goggles. Every single Hummer is filled with dozens of extra magazines of ammo for both weapons and a RPG-7D grenade launcher.

"They should be coming out of the club soon and everything is in place over there. So we're good to go," Primo, the driver, said to Luis.

"Good," he looked at a young couple kissing on the corner. "My God be with those in the way," Luis replied.

An hour later, a *CNN* news crew who was already stationed in Sonora covering the ongoing drug war for the past two weeks, is on the scene in Hermosillo reporting on what just took place.

"Steve, we can hear you now, go head," *CNN* news anchor, Bill Cooper, said.

"All right…as you can see, there are at least a hundred Mexican Federal Police and military officers, along with dozens of ambulances and fire trucks here on Boulevard Enrique between Talostitlan and Qjuelos Street. The carnage you see all over the street is from an intense gun battle that just took place a little while ago between the Rayon and La Perla Cartels that lasted at least an half an hour. I spoke to someone who witnessed the event unfold, and the person said that a convoy of thirty to forty black Hummers first ambushed the four cars you see there in the front, and then the three cars in the back that were incinerated with RPG grenade launchers. Then, about sixty of the La Perla members got out of the black Hummers and riddle all seven cars stuck in the middle of the incinerated ones with machine guns. Leaving, from what an officer told me was over six hundred cell casings on the streets. A total of thirty-eight Rayon Cartel members were killed along with their leader, Hector Santiago. We got word that the President of Mexico is going to hold a press conference in ten minutes regarding what just took place. One of the officers told me this is the biggest hit to ever take place in Mexico."

"They are crazy out there. Shit like that don't happen in America," Kia said to King as they sat at the breakfast bar in their kitchen watching *CNN* news coverage of what took place in Mexico just a couple of hours ago.

Not surprised at what happened, King shifts his eyes from the TV to the dinner table where his cell phone is vibrating.

"Hello."

"King, what's going on, my man?" Luis said, standing in his backyard of his mansion in Fajardo, Puerto Rico. "I told you things would change for the better and you looked at me like I was crazy when I told you that. But anyway...I'm here with Nando and Felix, and we'll be heading out there in a couple of days to meet with you. Okay, my man?"

"Not a problem," King replied, hanging up the phone and walking into the living room where Nicole is watching cartoons. Sitting down on the couch with her, King asked her what she wants Santa to get her for Christmas and her face lights up with the biggest smile as she tells him she has a list about a mile long. King couldn't help but laugh as she stares at him and says she's serious and pulls the list out of her pajama pocket.

"What in the world? Nicole, I know that's not a Christmas list? Who are you making wishes for? A small city in Africa, because all of that can't be just for you," Kia asked, sitting down next them.

"Daddy told me to make a list of everything I wanted for Christmas. So I wrote down everything I wanted Santa Claus to bring me," Nicole replied with a surprised look on her face.

"Yeah, but it's the front and back of the paper, Nicole. What are you going to do with all these toys?" Kia asked as she put her arm around Nicole and stared at the smile on her face.

"I'm going to play with all the toys, until next Christmas comes. Then I'm going to make another list."

*****

Parked on 21st Street in a black Tahoe, Agent Bauer watches as Flush walks toward him after talking to Fatal at the card tables inside the block. Rolling down the window and taking off his shades, Agent Bauer has a big smile on his face and calls Flush out by his real name. "Hey, Jason Rush…come over here, I need to talk to you."

"Fuck out of here, pig! I ain't talking to you," Flush replied, walking to his car.

"Pig! Bauer responded, hopping out of the car and approaching him. "I was wondering what you go by…Jason Rush or Damon Shaw?"

Stopping in his tracks and turning around with a confused look on his face. Flush stared at a white man in a suit that had just gotten out of the black Tahoe. Suddenly, Flush realized who he worked for.

"Yeah, you know who I work for so we can save the pleasantries. Just follow my car…we need to talk," Agent Bauer said to him.

Nervous and his heart racing at a hundred miles a minute, Flush follows Agent Bauer over the Pulaski Bridge to the Greenpoint sewage plant and they parked on Kingsland Avenue. Grabbing his Beretta out of his stash box and getting out his car, thoughts of killing Agent Bauer race through Flush's mind as he approaches the Tahoe.

"Don't even think about it; we are being watched right now. So get the thought out of your mind and get in."

"What the fuck do you want with me?"

"It's not you I want. I want your friend, King. I was reading your file. You've been working for us for three years now and have done a lot of good work for us. The two secret indictments that lead to fifty-two arrests, the Harris murder and some other shit…yeah, you've been good to us over the years and we have been good to you too. But I can't help but wonder why you haven't given up King yet; or even Haze, at that?"

"They're family, that's why. And for some reason, your bosses never asked me to."

"Well, not anymore. I know the Rayon used to supply him; now it's gonna be the La Perla after what happened earlier this morning in Mexico. I also know y'all are at war with the Italians right now and I know King had a bunch of other people murdered. Two of them were informants, just like you. Now you're gonna help me bring him down because it's only a matter of time before he finds out who you really are and kills you."

Flush knows he has no choice. The thought of giving King up has him scared shitless. Placing his head in his hands, he thinks back to the day he got arrested and how he should have just taken the time for the two guns and the credit card scam he was being charged with. But instead, he decided to help the FBI and had been able to continue running the streets ever since. "What's your plan 'cause I'm not wearing a wire; that shit's out of the question," Flush said.

"You won't need to, trust me."

After an hour of talking, Flush told Agent Bauer everything that's been going on over the past year. He also told him about the upcoming hit King had planned on Dominick Scalfani.

*****

"The one thing I hate is someone I can't trust. I killed a lot of people because I lost trust in them. Some of them thought they could take my spot and some decide to co-operate with the police against me," Luis explains to King, Nando and Felix as they all sit in Bogata, a Columbian lounge in East Elmhurst, Queens. "What we have now is the biggest drug operation in the world. Every cartel in Mexico has been calling me non-stop, wanting me to transport for them. Even the Colombians are showing interest. I'm in the process of building a super cartel ran by me and I want you to run the whole East Coast of America. In this position were in, with the CIA backing us, nobody is going to stop that from happening," Luis told King.

"The CIA? What the fuck are you talking about?" King asked, adjusting his body on the sofa.

"How the hell you think we're able to get all of these drugs into the country? It's not just by smuggling it on our own; we do this shit with the help of the CIA. It's been going on forever. It's called, The Ghost Connection. I've been working with them for ten years now," Nando told King.

The Ghost Connection is operation ran by a rouge unit of CIA agents that help transport heroin and cocaine into America for the drug cartels in exchange for money. The U.S. Government has made billions upon billions of dollars over the past decade smuggling drugs into America; which, in turn, they use the money to fund and start secret wars against Islamic extremist and radical groups.

"By this time next year, King, you'll be sitting on three hundred million dollars or more. That's just your profit. We're not just transporting the dope you're used to selling. We're adding cocaine and methamphetamine pills as well. We have to take advantage of the opportunities we have at our exposal to make as much money as we can, while we can. And we have the first shipment arriving in five days. It's two tons of dope, one ton of cocaine, and 250 pounds of methamphetamine pills. Don't worry about moving the pills for now; Nando and Felix are going to handle that. They already have some buyers, so they'll introduce you to them in due time," Luis said.

Sitting back and processing the thought of making three hundred million dollars or more in just a year, and knowing there's gonna be more bloodshed and more boroughs to take over, he doesn't think twice.

"I'mma do this one year run with y'all and then I'm handing it all over to Haze and stepping out of the limelight. He's gonna run the day-to-day operations and I will be in the background. You can trust him, he's my brother and he's been very loyal to me."

"Not a problem, but let's get through the first year and then we can discuss all that. Right now we need to stay on point and make this money. Too much success," Luis said, lifting his glass in the air as they all toast.

Five days later

Haze watches as two of his soldiers open the gate so the three Red Cross vans can pull in to the medical warehouse owned by him on Old Country Road in Westbury, NY. Haze's eyes light up as the drivers open the vans up and he sees a hundred and ninety million dollars' worth of drugs. Unloading the drugs out the vans, the workers divide them in ten white Toyota Prius Hybrid cars

218

with the words, *AXT Laboratory Transport* on both sides of the car. It's a cover company Haze started to transport the drugs into the city without too much hassle from the cops.

"Listen…these four cars go to Nando's storage in Flushing, and place the rest of the pills over there in those two vans. You already know where the other six cars go; make sure they get there before 10:00 p.m. You got me?" Haze said to his transport supervisor.

Good look, are the words King reads off the text message Haze just sent him regarding the shipment. Standing in the middle of the dance floor looking over to the bar area, King isn't satisfied with the lighting above the bar. He thinks it is too bright. King is hell bent on making sure that the lounge will be ready to open on New Year's Eve.

"Flush, do those lights over the bar look too bright to you?" King asked him.

"Nah, they look just right."

"Of course it looks just right to you; you've got on sunglasses. Take them shits off and look," King told him. His eyes squinted as he stared at Flush, noticing that his eyes are bloodshot red. "What the fuck you on…coke, nigga?"

"Nah, fam…you wilding right now."

"Why the fuck you got the coke face then? I can't ask you shit right now, B."

Leaning up against his Hummer and pulling off of a cigar, King stares at the long, red awning outside of the lounge with the name Black Roses on it in black and red letters. He can't help but think how Haze is the only strong-minded person he has left that's down with him.

"King, everything all right?" a short, middle-aged Italian man named Frank who is the contractor of the project asked.

"Yeah, I'm just hoping it will be done in time."

"Every time you hire me to do a job, don't I get it done in time? It will be done, and ready to open for New Year's Eve; don't worry about it. Trust me. What you need to be worried about is the coffee shop reopening. I know your losing a lot of money from that."

"Yeah, I've lost about $60,000 since it's been closed; but it's coming along. Next week it will reopen. The city tried to postpone it, but they lost that battle."

"The city always does shit like that," Frank said, pulling out a cigarette.

"Oh, yeah…I forgot to thank you for the flowers for Mel and Tone's wakes. Kia told me they were from your company," King said.

"I really liked Mel and Tone...they were cool dudes. They would always tell me funny stories about you and them; especially the one about when y'all were in Las Vegas."

"They actually told you about that? Jesus Christ, them motherfucker's had big mouths. They told you their version; not the real one."

Shaking his head, but smiling at the same time, King realizes just how much he misses them, even though he tries to block it out and move on.

"Well, it's Christmas Eve and I have to get home to the family before they kill me. Enjoy your Christmas and make sure you take the gifts I left in your office for Kia and Nicole with you," Frank told him, giving him a hug.

"I won't forget. Nicole will kill me if I forgot Uncle Frank's gift," King said, laughing and walking into the lounge.

*****

Waking up to the sound of her alarm clock that she had set for 8:00 a.m., joy overwhelms her as she gets up and runs into her bathroom and brushes her teeth and washes her face. Running down the stairs and into the living room, she stares at all the presents under the big white Christmas tree and a smile comes across her face. Walking over to the tree, Nicole sees that almost every present under the tree has her name on it; making her chuckle with excitement. Running back up the stairs and cracking open her parents' bedroom door, she tip toes in and opens up the drapes. The sun shines through the bedroom, causing King to wake up as Nicole jumps on the bed, yelling, "Merry Christmas."

"Ya'll are going to let the whole day go by. You're missing all the fun. It's time to get up and open up presents," she said to her parents, walking out the bedroom and back downstairs.

Sitting on the couch together drinking coffee, King and Kia watched Nicole unwrap every gift she wanted on her list. Getting up after unwrapping the last gift, Nicole told them she has a gift for each of them and runs upstairs to get them.

"This is for you and this is for you," she said as she hands her parents their gifts. "Don't worry about the wrapping; I'm not good at that yet."

Kia and King both un-wrap their gifts and Kia pulls out a red and black Louis Vuitton scarf with the matching wool hat that she's been wanting to get for a long time.

King pulls out a beige Tom Ford dress shirt and a tie to match.

"Nicole, who bought these for you? That's not the gift we bought together for you to give to your father."

"Uncle Tone went and got them for me the day before he passed away."

Closing his eyes, overwhelmed with emotion, King whispered, *Thank you,* into the air to Tone and then opened his eyes back up to the sight of Kia hugging Nicole as tears fall down her face.

"There's one more gift that mommy has to open," King said, reaching into his bathrobe pocket and pulling out a small box and getting down on one knee.

CHAPTER 11

"Boom! Boom! Boom! Death comes in threes, my
man."

~Carmine Assante

"Will you marry me?"

After ten long years, the moment she's been waiting
for finally had arrived. Without any hesitation or even
looking at the beautiful and eight-carat diamond ring, Kia
said yes and Nicole jumped up and down, clapping her
hands; excited and watching her parents hug and kiss.

"Well, congratulations to the newly-engaged
couple," Agent Crebbs said as he and Agent Donaldson sit
in a van parked on Bacon Road up the block from King's
house. "Flush, put the bug in a good place in the living
room. Now we just gotta see how the one in the basement
picks up."

Helping King wrap all of Nicole presents the night
before, Flush was able to plant two bugs inside the house;
one in the living room and one in the basement. Filled with
guilt while he was doing it, he didn't realize that Nicole had
woken up from her sleep from the noise of the wrapping
paper and sneaked out of her room and saw him from the

224

living room balcony, replacing the baseball on top of the fireplace with another one while King was in the bathroom.

"The French toast is good, mommy," Nicole said as she and King ate at the breakfast bar. Daddy, I forgot to ask you why Uncle Flush changed your favorite baseball on the fireplace," she whispers to him.

"What are you talking about? He changed my baseball?"

"That's a new ball up there; I saw him do it when y'all were wrapping gifts the other night."

Taking a sip from his coffee cup and staring at the baseball, only one thing runs through King's mind. *This nigga planted a bug in my house,* he said to himself. Getting up and walking over to the fireplace, King grabs the ball and feels how light it is. Immediately he knows it's not his baseball and just one that has been hollowed out on the inside.

Walking downstairs to the basement and grabbing a saw from his tool shed, he takes a seat at the card table and begins to cut open the baseball. The sight of the small black listing device enrages King as he smashes it against the table. *Fuck!* he said to himself as he realizes there's also a bug somewhere in the basement because they came down there that night after wrapping the gifts.

Leaning back in the chair, King tries to digest the new turn of events that he's been faced with. Thinking to himself, *This motherfucker knew I just got the house swept the day before he came over, and he knew that I called a meeting tonight down here for the hit tomorrow on Dom. God damn, this nigga told the FBI everything,* he cracks a slight smile.

"The mic in the living room just went out after I heard a shaking sound from the mic in the baseball and then a smashing sound off of the mic in the basement," Agent Crebbs told agent Donaldson.

"Shit, how the fuck did he know that the baseball had a bug in it? Fuck, he's going to cancel the meeting tonight. I'm going to call Sam. Flush's cover might be blown," Agent Donaldson said.

What the fuck happened now, Haze said to himself as he reads the text message.

Meet me in thirty minutes...light, King sent the message as he got into his car.

It's always something with this nigga. I can't even enjoy Christmas with my bitch right now. I swear to God this shit better be important, Haze said to himself, driving down 21st Street.

Pulling into the parking lot of the light house on Roosevelt Island, Haze sees the anger on King's face as he steps out of the car and walks toward him.

"What happened, fam?"

"What happened is that Flush planted bugs in my house for the FBI. I found one this morning. That nigga is a fucking rat. Nicole told me she saw Flush switch my Yankee's baseball on top of the fireplace with another one that looked identical to it. I cut the shit open, and there's nothing inside except for a fucking mic in it."

"What the fuck? Flush did that? I can't believe it," Haze said, putting his hand on his head, shocked at what he was hearing.

"There has to be another one somewhere in the basement because we chilled down there also. Lord knows what he told them or how long ago they turned him and where else he has planted bugs. There could be one in the shop, your loft, any fucking where. Who the fuck knows? Cancel the thing for tomorrow and move everything to the new spots immediately."

"I'll handle it, don't worry. But damn, fam…on Christmas Day we find out Flush is a rat. It's crazy; you can't even trust the niggas that's the closest to you anymore, and now there are only two of us left."

You're right, King said to himself, staring at Haze as he looks off into the sky at the helicopter passing by. "Kill that rat motherfucker and dump him in the acid barrel," King said, giving Haze a pound and then getting in his car.

Driving on the Grand Central Parkway back home, King starts to contemplate if he can really trust Haze now; even though Haze has been nothing but loyal to him and never shown him a reason to think otherwise, the thought still lingers in his mind. He remembers the story Hector Santiago once told him about how he had to kill some of his own family members that helped him on his rise to power, just because he couldn't trust them any more...even if they were still loyal.

*****

FBI Headquarters
26 Federal Plaza - 7th floor
Manhattan, New York

"He definitely deaded the meeting tonight and the hit on Dominick Sclafani if he found the bug in the baseball. Or maybe, he or his daughter might have just thrown the baseball against the wall or something and he does not know that the bug exists. We don't know for certain yet. Did you tell Flush that King might have found out?" Agent Bauer asked Agent Mackey.

"He's not answering his phone. I've been calling him since the mic went dead."

"All right, we just gotta wait and..." he stops mid-sentence and answers his cell phone. What's up, Donaldson? Great...call me if anything else happens," Bauer ends his call. "Donaldson said he heard King over the basement mic pissed off that Nicole was playing with the baseball down there. So it looks like he didn't find out, unless King is fucking with us."

"Well, we'll see if he still has the meeting tonight and he's not bull shitting; dragging us along," Agent Mackey said.

"I pray to God he's not; having him on tape ordering the hit on Dominick Sclafani is what we need. Who knows what else he will talk about down there, and did y'all finish getting all the equipment over to the apartment across the street from the lounge?"

"Yeah, everything is setup over there. Crebbs finished up this morning," Agent Mackey replied.

"Good, we can start doing surveillance then."

"Well, what do you know? This is Flush right here calling me," Agent Mackey said as he answers his phone.

After being picked up by Haze and told that the meeting was canceled because King had to fly out to Miami for an urgent meeting with Luis, Haze took Flush to his warehouse in Westbury, NY. He told him he had a big-time card game setup for the night since the meeting had been canceled. Flush thought something was wrong and his cover was blown when Haze came to pick him up and told him that. But when he saw Gotti and Hoffa show up to ride along with them, he thought he was in the clear and everything was exactly as Haze said it was and that King hadn't found out what he had done.

As they walked through the door of the warehouse which is normally filled with the company cars they used to transport their drugs in and a couple of desks and tables, it's completely empty. Flush's eyes widened as the only thing he sees is a couple of chains hanging from the ceiling down to the floor in the middle of the warehouse. His stomach turns, realizing there was no card game set-up, and before he could turn around, Haze smacked him in the back of the head with his gun, knocking him out cold. Hanging from the chains with his body stripped naked, Flush opened his eyes to Haze standing in front of him with the scariest grin on his face as he held a metal baseball bat.

"Haze, I didn't tell on you. I swear. All the Feds want is King. Please don't do this, please," Flush said to Haze as tears started to fall down his face. "Please don't do this, Haze...I'm begging you. You could run everything if they get King."

The sight of Flush begging for forgiveness for what he did made Haze even more angry, and before Flush could say another word, Haze swung the metal bat connecting with the left side of his ribs, shattering two of them. Haze didn't stop there, he just keep beating his ribs and his legs with the bat as if he was a human piñata, as Flush loud pleads for Haze to stop echoed off the walls of the empty warehouse. The torture didn't stop there as Hoffa curved the word *rat* into Flush's stomach with an army knife slowly, as Flush started to urinate on himself from the pain. Opening his eyes after passing out for a couple of minutes, Flush watches as Gotti, dressed in a blue hazmat suit, wheels the big, gray acid barrel over to him.

"Haze, please don't do this. I told you, I didn't give you up; all they want is King," Flush told him in an exhausted tone.

"You rat motherfucker!" Haze said with a disgusted look on his face as he gripped the baseball bat tighter. "After all that we have done for you, this is how you repay us? You give us up to the fucking Feds? You're running around with us and yet you're working for them pigs. Why couldn't you just do the fucking time for what they had you on, instead of snitching?"

"Man, fuck all this talking! Let's kill this nigga and get out of here," Hoffa told Haze in an impatient tone.

"You know what...do this one thing for me and I might let you live," Haze said to Flush, pulling out his cell phone.

Staring at Hoffa and Gotti's faces, Flush knew Haze was lying and wasn't gonna let him live. So Flush agreed to make the call because he knew if he didn't, they would just keep torturing him and he couldn't take it anymore. He just wanted to die.

Hanging up the phone, Haze cracked a smile at Flush and nodded to him, telling him that he had done well, and then he put a bullet through his head. As Gotti opens the top of the barrel, Hoffa raises Flush's body over it and then slowly pulls on the chains lowering his body as they put on gas masks and watch his body disintegrate.

"We gotta stop and get something to eat 'cause I'm starving right now," Gotti said as the three of them got in his Cadillac Truck and head back to Queens.

"How the fuck can you eat after doing that shit?" Hoffa asked Gotti.

"What? You got a soft stomach nigga? When I'm hungry, I'm hungry; killing ain't got shit to do with that," Gotti replied with a smirk on his face, watching Hoffa shake his head.

As Gotti and Hoffa kept snapping on each other on the ride back to Queens, Haze started to wonder about everything Flush had told him. From how much the Feds already knew along with what he told Agent Bauer, to how badly they wanted King.

*****

King and Frank, the contractor, stood outside; staring at the finished Black Roses Lounge with smiles on their faces and proud with the outcome of the work done to it. It cost $250,000 for King to merge both storefronts together and renovate them into the lounge.

"I told you it would be done; didn't I?" Frank said to King, giving him a hug.

"You did; you gave me your word and it's done in time. The place is amazing. I'll wire you an extra twenty grand for this; consider it a bonus. You and your team did a great job, Frank."

"You should gross $150,000 to $200,000 a month off this place, easy," Frank stated.

"I hope so," King replied as he pulled out his phone and started taking pictures of the inside of the lounge and the outside. He sent them to Kia and Haze.

Staked out across the street in the second floor apartment located in a three-story apartment building across the street from the lounge is agent Mackey, Crebbs and Donaldson. Taking pictures and doing video surveillance, they informed Agent Bauer that Flush was not at the lounge and still hadn't picked up his phone. That led them to believe that King had found out about the bugs and had him killed. That's why the meeting never took place last night as they waited for four hours listening to the silence in King's basement. It was going on 6:00 p.m. and Dominick Sclafani was still alive.

"King found out and now were right back where we started," Agent Mackey said, staring at King taking pictures of the outside of the lounge.

"We'll find a way to get him. If not...the Italians will probably kill him. He's not going to get away with killing a mob boss and high ranking captains. That's just not happening; especially with crazy ass, trigger-happy Carmine out there," Agent Crebbs stated.

"You might be right; but the way it looks, King doesn't give a fuck that they're the mob. He has more than enough money to fight them and the resources," Agent Mackey said, getting up and walking out the room.

The sound of Sinatra's voice blasts through the speakers of Carmine's Porsche as he sings along to the song, *That's Life*. He was waiting for Sunny, one of his soldiers, to come out of the gambling spot on Troy and Atlantic Avenue in Brooklyn. It's a new spot Carmine opened up without Dom's permission and it's been bringing in a lot of money. Knowing Dom has a hit out on him; Carmine has been out in the open all over Brooklyn instead of laying low like he was advised to do by the other captains that are on his side in this beef.

"Everything there? The whole thirty grand?" Carmine asked as Sunny nodded his head and handed him a yellow envelope.

"This spot has been making a lot of money in the past two weeks. I'm surprised Dom hasn't tried to hit it," Sunny said.

"He's not worried about this spot. Trust me. I found out he brought some friends of ours over from the homeland to take me out. He doesn't even have faith in his own soldiers to do the job."

"You gotta hit first. That plan you came up with could work. It's crazy...but fuck it. It's old school Cosa Nostra for real," Sunny stated.

"It is out in the open...on front street for the world to see. But first, we gotta handle the other problem we have. I got some information on him so it should be easy. Because Dom isn't handling it right. So, I'm going to kill King myself and then I want you to send the Lepke twins after that other snake motherfucker, and then we take care of Dom. *Boom! Boom! Boom!* Death comes in threes, my man," Carmine said with a big smile on his face.

"Fino alla morte, (*Italian for, Until death*)" Sunny replied.

*****

FBI Headquarters

26 Federal Plaza - 7th floor

Manhattan, New York

"Listen up everybody. Let me have your attention," Agent Bauer ordered, standing in front of the packed conference room full of agents. "We've lost all contact with Jason Rush, aka Flush, and he is nowhere to be found as of right now. We believe King might have found out about our plan and had him killed; we don't know yet, but we can't take any more chances on it. So, I wanna do sweeps on every location we've been watching in Queens and the Bronx. Start rounding up all of the low-level workers in his organization. Out of all these suspects we have targeted, somebody's gonna talk; they don't all love King."

"6:00 a.m. tomorrow morning is the time we hit every spot. So everyone is to report here at 4:00 a.m.," he looks at his watch, "…which is in eleven hours from now and we'll break into units and move out," Agent Mackey said to the other agents.

"Mackey, our unit is gonna hit Queensbridge and Ravenswood Projects; Donaldson's unit will hit the Bronx locations, and Crebbs unit will hit Skillman Avenue locations," Agent Bauer told him, as they walked out of the conference room and into his office.

"All right, I'll let them know in the morning. I just hope some of these motherfuckers out of the sixty that we are rounding up, talk," Agent Mackey replied.

"Someone will talk; they always do. And what the fuck does he want now?" Agent Bauer said looking at one of the heads of the FBI, Agent Abbott, walking toward his office.

Dozens of cars and vans arrived at the locations in Queens and the Bronx at 6:00 a.m. on the dot, as they planned. The FBI swept every location they had under surveillance due to the information Flush had provided. Stash houses, Bodegas, several apartments and two storage facilities. They arrested fifty-three out of the sixty suspects they had targeted. From all the locations combined, they recovered over 5.8 million dollars in cash, five hundred and twenty pounds of heroin, three hundred and seventy pounds of cocaine, thirty pounds of marijuana and thirty-three guns.

King's phone blew up as soon as the sweeps took place. He knew Flush had given the FBI the locations; but they weren't the real money spots and stash houses. Flush didn't know where those were. King had no worries;

whatever the FBI took he knew he could get back, plus more. Knowing the FBI had nothing on him because he never dealt with the people they arrested and they still didn't have anything else to implicate him in any wrong doing, he just continued to sit in his living room as he watched the breaking news on *NY1* and drank his cup of coffee before heading over to the lounge.

Agent Bauer and his team interrogated every single suspect trying to get one of them to crack and give them anything on King and Haze. The majority of the suspects refused to talk; they were willing to do the time instead of snitching. But Agent Bauer caught a break when two suspects from the Skillman Avenue Crew, told him that something major was gonna go down at King's lounge at his New Year's Eve party. They didn't know what it was, but they overheard their leader, Danny Boy, talking about it.

*****

The smoke from his Lano Estate cigar bounces off of the red walls of the office as he sits on the edge of his custom-made, all black with red trim Versace desk, watching Haze put silk Versace shirts in the closet.

"The office is official right; better than the one at Roses?" King asked him.

"Yeah, fam…it definitely is. It's bigger."

"I forgot to tell you me and Kia are engaged. I proposed to her Christmas morning."

"Congrats, my nigga," Haze gives him a hug. "Why you didn't you tell me when I saw you that day?"

"The shit with our old homie made me forget to tell you. I forgot all about it once I found the bug. After I left you, I had the whole crib swept and they found the second bug he put in the basement. He put it behind the little picture frame that's on the table, right beside the couch."

"He was always a sneaky motherfucker," Haze said, letting out a slight laugh and shaking his head.

"By the way, what happened with that? He was crying, asking you to let him live?" King asked.

"You know he was. He also said FBI Agent Sam Bauer wants you and me bad. The agent just found out; homie turned rat a couple of years ago, after he got popped for two guns and some credit card scam with his girl. So he was using him. Flush told them everything; murders, our dealings with the Rayon Cartel, and the beef with the Italians; but there's no proof. So they were focused on the beef with the Italians and the meeting we were supposed to have that night. That's why he planted the bugs. He didn't tell me…but I'm sure he told them about them spots that got swept. So, since the meeting didn't happen, they hit the spots."

Cracking a smile and leaning back in his chair, King realizes that Agent Bauer is gonna be a problem that Luis Beltre is going to have to handle for him.

"King, you know that was a big loss we took today and the other thing we had planned got delayed. Those spots are dead now and we lost a lot of workers. So we gonna start losing a little more money 'cause of it. And we still got the Dom situation we gotta deal with."

"As far as the Italian, he's gonna be dealt with. Don't worry about that, just worry about what you gotta handle. And the other thing that happened this morning… that shit won't break us. They ain't got shit on us and the motherfuckers they snatched up don't know shit; Flush dealt with all them people anyway. Whatever we lost, we'll get back. Trust me. We gonna be rich forever."

"Excuse me, King…there's an FBI agent here named Mr. Bauer that's out front looking for you. Denise told him you weren't here, but he's not leaving," Monica, one of the lounge's bartenders, told him.

A look of shock appears on King and Haze's faces. "It's okay; tell Mr. Bauer I'll be out in two minutes," King replied.

"The balls on this motherfucker to show up here after the shit he pulled," Haze said, shaking his head.

"It's cool. I wanna meet the man that's trying to bring me down," King replied, putting on his beige blazer and walking out the office.

Walking into the lounge, King cracks a smile staring at the white man standing at the bar dressed in the same gray and blue pin-striped Givenchy suit that King has at home.

"The modern day J. Edgar Hoover is in my lounge. Mr. Bauer, either you have really great taste or you had those two agents that are parked up the block from my house, sneak in my house and take that suit from my closet and give it to you," King said jokingly with a smile on his face and extending his hand.

Agent Bauer felt like spitting on King's hand instead of shaking it; but he did neither. "I know what you did to Flush and everything else you been doing over the past year. He told me everything. You honestly think you're gonna continue to get away with the shit you're doing out here?"

"Absolutely. If the stock market continues to keep going the way it's been for the past year and I can continue to open up businesses…why not? It's the American way, right," King replied.

Shaking his head and letting out a slight laugh, Agent Bauer responds, "I've been at the agency for twenty years and your case is by far the hardest case I ever worked on. You're a smart man; I'll give you that, but everything rotten comes to an end. You and I both know that. You're not the kind-hearted family man you portray yourself to be. You're a murderer, a drug lord, and a menace to society. That's what you are," Agent Bauer said, looking into King's eyes and seeing no emotion.

King didn't say anything; he just stared at the middle-aged Irish agent with blond hair and blue eyes, as he ran his mouth.

"Just take look around you, what do you have left? Everybody's gone; it's only you and Haze left and can you really trust him now? Can you trust anybody that works for you in your organization?"

"Listen, Mr. Bauer…and please don't take it personally. I could care less how long you've been on your job, and what you think I do and what you think you know. All I know is until you have something to arrest me on, I'm free to live my life as the businessman that I am. So, it was a pleasure meeting you and don't ever show up at my places of business again unless you're coming to arrest me," King said in an aggressive tone and then turned around and walked back to his office.

CHAPTER 12

"It's gonna be taken care of tonight."

~Nando Sanchez

"Felix, you should try the other Tequila; it's stronger. Believe me, drink that shit and you'll be waking up in Columbia in a coke field in Bogota," Luis said as he, Felix and Nando sat on his one hundred and seventy-five foot luxury yacht as it cruises the Caribbean Sea. "Nando, I forgot to ask you how much in total was left in those storages in Hermosillo?" Luis asked.

"Not that much; it was a little over two tons of heroin and three tons of cocaine. It's already on its way to New York since the FBI hit a bunch of King's spots earlier this morning," Nando replied.

Not satisfied with what he heard, but not upset, Luis thought there would have been more drugs since the Rayon was labeled the richest cartel in Mexico. He figured the remaining members that he didn't kill that night would hit the storages and money houses, taking everything they could.

"All right, we have a shipment coming in from the Colombians on Wednesday morning in La Perla. It's a big one; four tons of heroin. So I need y'all to be there with my brothers to make sure it's right. I paid the Colombians in advance and I don't want them fuckin' shorting me," Luis told Nando and Felix.

"Not a problem. Felix and I will be there for the shipment," Nando replied.

"Then on Thursday, I need the two of you in Sonora to meet with the heads of the Juarez and Ciudad Cartels. They are having second thoughts about doing business with me for some reason. I don't feel like waging war against them right now; so convince them it's better for us to do business than be on opposite sides right now," Luis told Nando and Felix, and then opened up the custom-made Oakwood cigar box on the table that was filled with twenty Lano Estate cigars. "These cigars are from King," he hands one to Nando and then Felix. "He gave them to me as a gift. Limited edition Lano Estate made just for me. And how is my friend King doing with that problem he has with the Italians?"

"It's gonna be taken care of tonight," Nando replied.

Covering his head with his leather jacket to protect himself from the rain pouring down, King runs into Betony restaurant on 53rd Street in midtown Manhattan. It is regarded as one of the best restaurants in New York City.

King eats there at least once a week. Walking in and being escorted to his usual table upstairs in the back of the restaurant, King notices that the restaurant is damn near empty. Taking a seat, his usual roasted chicken Salsify and perigord truffles, and a bottle of Chateau Montelena 2007 are already waiting for him.

Halfway through his meal, King notices three well-dressed Italian men being escorted by the hostess up the stairs. He pulls out his Glock 9mm and holds it under the table, watching the three men take their seats at the table directly across from him.

Getting up from the table, the clean shaven, baby-faced Italian walks over to King's table. He puts both of his hands up and slowly opens his beige suit jacket to show King that he's not carrying. King notions with his hand, telling him to take a seat. Placing his gun beside him on the leather seat; King wipes his mouth with a napkin before motioning for the man to speak.

"So, you're the motherfucker that had them cunts kill my cousin, Sal," Leaning forward in his seat he continues, "It was smart; I give you that. But the spic that ordered it, Nando, called me and told me there was a reason for it and it had to be done. So he told me to meet with you. So now I'm here and what's the fucking reason?"

"Big Sal was running your family and this city while working as an informant for the FBI. He thought they would protect him and no one would find out, like all informants think. You can't do business with a Mexican Cartel and think they won't eventually find out. He thought he was invincible."

"What! You think I'm some fucking Giamope? (*Italian for, idiot*). What makes you think that I'm supposed to believe that? My cousin was no fucking rat! Ratting doesn't run in my blood line."

"Let me show you something," King said, grabbing his phone off of the table. "The only reason I got this picture in my phone is because I thought it might convince you. Other than that, I got rid of every picture I have of me and him; Nando told me he was an informant. I didn't believe him at first and then he showed me the proof. He's right here," King said, showing Carmine the picture.

"I saw the news coverage of it after it happened. It was in all the papers," Carmine said and then leaned back in his chair.

"He was my mentor in these streets; but he was a fucking rat. His name was Mac. He ran Queens for years. Nobody knew, but he was setting his own workers up, giving information on other niggas throughout Queens.

And he started to give information on Nando and his boss. He thought he could retire from the streets and move away without anyone finding out. But the streets weren't done with him. So I told Nando I'd be more than happy to take care of him myself. I wouldn't have taken the hit on your cousin if it wasn't legit. I give you my word."

Convinced of what he just heard, and soaking in the fact that his cousin was a rat, Carmine pulls out a pack of Newports and calls the waitress over, letting her know to bring him another bottle of what King had. Lighting up a cigarette, he sees King looking at him as if he had done something wrong.

"What, I'm a partner in this restaurant. I can smoke in here if I want to. If you wanna smoke, go ahead," Carmine told King and King grabs a cigar out of his coat pocket.

"Don't put too much trust in friends. That's one of the laws. But I didn't think my cousin would be a rat. The most powerful family in New York, and the boss was a rat. And now this old fuck runs the family and he probably knew Sal was a rat," Carmine said, pouring himself a glass of the Chateau Montelena. "I'll talk to the captains that are still loyal to me and make sure whatever retaliation my family had planned, is called off. So there's no more bloodshed."

"Well, it seems like you have a legit reason to have a change in your family. I'm just saying."

"I understand. The old fuck has a hit on me as we speak. But it seems like there's another legit reason that you might have to make a change in your family."

Taking a pull from his cigar and wondering what Carmine is talking about, the hairs on the back of King's neck stand up awaiting what Carmine was about to say.

"Your second in charge, Haze. I call him the snake. He's been reaching out to my family to have you killed. He called me just the other day, giving me your home address, your plate numbers and where you would be."

"Get the fuck out of here! Haze has been calling your family to have me killed?" Dumping the cigar ashes into the ashtray and letting out a slight laugh, King is shocked, but not surprised. He had been having doubts about Haze, but had been trying to put them out of his mind. King's nerves start to get jumpy and his blood starts boiling thinking about it.

"He called Sal before he was killed that night and let him know you took the contract on him. He and my new boss, Dom, set up the hit that Sunday afternoon when you went to pick up your family up at the ice cream shop. Now the shooters were supposed to have back down that day because your girl and daughter were there; but Dom hired amateurs and they did what they wanted to do. And let's not forget about the car bomb. One of our captains got Haze the C4 and he planted it and detonated it. That was all him. I'm sorry to tell you, but it's all true."

Remaining calm, but furious on the inside, King remembers Haze had a phone in his hand, standing at the counter in the coffee shop when the car blew up. Then that Sunday afternoon before he went to pick up Kia and Nicole, he remembers Haze barley talked to him when he was there watching the football game. King fantasizes of how he's going to torture Haze before he kills him for even gaining the heart to go against him and do what he did.

"I'm shocked, but I'm not surprised. Being in my position, nothing surprises you anymore. Crew members snitching, stealing, and others plot against you to take your spot. It always happens; you just gotta catch it before your lights go out. I owe you for telling me this when we both know you didn't have to."

"I didn't plan on it. Trust me. I was coming here to sit down and listen to what you had to say and then I was gonna have them two zips over there blow your head off. But I believe what you have told me, for some reason. And I don't like that prick, Haze; something about him rubs me the wrong way. That's why I told you."

The doors of the restaurant were closed for the night and King and Carmine were still at the table for two more hours, drinking, telling stories and sharing business ideas; getting to know each other and finding out they had more in common with each other than they realized.

CHAPTER 13

"Fuck it, plan B."

~King

New Year's Eve

Monday, December 31, 12:30 p.m.

"Nicole, why you got the TV up so loud and you're not even watching it? Kia said irritated at the fact that Nicole does it all the time, just like her father. "How many times do I have to keep telling you to stop doing that; you're going to go deaf."

"I was listening to it while I was drawing. Daddy's gonna be home soon and he's gonna have it louder than that," she said, throwing her hands in the air and turning back around; continuing to draw.

Knowing her mother is gonna come after her, she gets up before Kia could get to her and dashes to the kitchen. Ducking and dodging her mother, Nicole makes it upstairs to her bedroom and hides in her closet. The sound of chairs being moved and the sheets on her bed being taking off, Nicole lets out a slight chuckle thinking her mother doesn't know where she's hiding. The sound of Kia's footsteps and the bedroom door closing makes Nicole think her mother has left the room. So as soon as she opens up the closet, Kia pulls her out and throws her over her shoulder and carries her downstairs. Laughing hysterically, Nicole says she's sorry, as King and S walk through the front door. She screams for her father and cousin to help her.

"Hey, where are you going with my daughter?" King said in a playful voice. "I brought some Outback for us to eat before your sister comes over to pick her up at three o'clock."

"Put me down, mommy; daddy got the blooming onion for us and some ribs. Come on."

Putting Nicole down and watching her run to the kitchen table makes her laugh, knowing how much her babygirl loves Outback. "You're lucky your father came home, 'cause I was gonna beat you up. And how you take the whole onion for yourself? You better split that in half, girl."

They all sit down and enjoy the meal before they start getting Nicole ready to leave and spend New Year's Eve with her cousins and her aunt.

Sitting in the basement after Lisa came and picked up Nicole and Kia's hair stylist came over, King explained to S the information he was told about Haze from Carmine Assante and how he's gonna handle the situation.

"So, Gotti and Hoffa are helping him out?" S asked.

"They are the only people crazy enough to ride with him. I'm pretty sure he told Gotti I was behind the Biz and Kev hit. So, it was easy to for him to pull Gotti in. Plus, Haze has a loyalty to Hoffa, because he came up under him, and the only reason Hoffa is on the streets right now is because of Haze. So, he's owes Him. Also Nando called me this morning and told me a shipment at his warehouse was ambushed and three of his men were killed this morning. It was them motherfuckers that did it, because Haze still hasn't called me to let me know what happened. So, I'm pretty sure his plan is to kill me tonight at the party or shortly after it," King replied.

S shook his head in disbelief and was enraged that Haze had actually killed Mel and Tone and set King up; almost killing Nicole and Kia in the process.

"And since he's trying to kill me, he told Gotti you killed Biz and Kev so Gotti has a plan to hit you too," King told him.

"I know that, fam. He knows he gotta kill me. No matter who killed you, if it was him or some other beef you got, he knows I'm killing him just off GP. But why the fuck is he doing this? The nigga just got power hungry out of nowhere or was there a problem between y'all lying dormant all along?"

"Haze knows as long as I'm alive, he's never gonna have one hundred percent control over everything; even if I put him in charge. And the amount of money we're about to make with Luis Beltre…shittttt! So, if they take me out, New York is all theirs. All the hard work has been done already; there's no other crews standing in their way out here in Queens. And we wholesale to every other big time crew in the other boroughs. Killing me makes sense to him because everything would be his and the shit is all set up for the nigga to be on top if I'm gone."

"This shit just sounds crazy, fam. Those niggas are on some other shit and really don't know who they are fucking with!" S stated, staring his cousin in the eyes and noticing how calm he was considering the fact that he was about to kill the last remaining member of his crew.

"It's my fault. I raised both of them motherfuckers to be this way," King said, rubbing his forehead.

"Fam, you taught Haze and Gotti how to get real money and survive out here just like you taught me. But you didn't teach us to how to become snakes. That's some shit that they already must have had inside them, my nigga. That's shit you're born with, you don't learn."

King let out a slight laugh, he knew what his cousin said was right. He just felt guilty at the moment for what was happening. "We're gonna leave together; but me and Kia gonna show up ten minutes after you. I want you to check it out first and have a couple of your niggas inside and on the low outside before we even leave here."

The hours went by and King explained to S his plan. S thought his plan was beyond reckless, but he agreed with his cousin and had his back no matter what he decided. So S set everything up as he was instructed to do, and then they started to get ready along with Kia for the party.

As he pulled up to the apartment building across the street from Black Roses Lounge, Agent Bauer felt overly confident, thinking that tonight would be the night something would happen and he could finally close the chapter on King.

"Everything is working properly. The Cameras, monitors, there's no feedback on the audio sound from the wires on our two agents, and the video feed from the cameras in their bow ties are perfect. There are two units outside; one up the block and the other down the block. And there's a unit at King's house now. So we're good to go, baby," Agent Donaldson said to Agent Bauer, giving him a high five.

"Mackey, put a smile on your face. It's going down tonight," Agent Bauer said to him, seeing how upset he is that he has to work on New Year's Eve.

"I would be smiling if I was at my house with my family with a New Year's hat on and drunk off my ass on motherfuckin' Tequila!" Agent Mackey screamed out loud.

"All y'all need to do is just stay in the vicinity of King and Haze. We hacked into Haze's computer and put y'all on the guest list so the security guards shouldn't give you a hard time," Agent Bauer said to the two agents, ready to go across the street to the lounge.

As ten o'clock rolled around, people have started to show up to the lounge; they parked their Bentleys, Maserati's and other luxury cars up and down the streets of Vernon Boulevard. Agent Bauer and the other agents watched on the surveillance monitors as people took pictures on the red carpet outside the lounge before they went in, dressed in designer clothes from head to toe and wearing minks and all different types of furs.

It's New Year's Eve and it's about forty-five minutes before the ball drops; the lounge is packed with people. Bottles of Dom Perignon, Patron and Hennessy sit in black and gold buckets filled with ice on every table throughout the lounge. Heavy cigar smoke lingers in the air as sexy women along with a who's who list of ballplayers, celebrities, rappers, and close friends and business associates of King take up every inch of vacant space in the lounge. The joint is on point and everyone is ready to bring in the new year in with a bang while celebrating the grand opening of the lounge.

Walking through the front door, the appearance of the lounge has a modern and welcoming feel to it. LED ceiling panel lights in red, gold and black with custom-made decorations and mirrored framing cover the ceiling throughout the majority of the lounge. It has a spacious L-shaped bar area, with a black marble granite counter top. Three bartenders and six waitresses work the main area and more than one hundred different liquors and wines align the back wall of the bar. Two 65-inch 4K-ultra flat screen TVs hang from the ceiling above the bar; visible from any seat in the lounge. There's also a nice sized VIP area were the lighting from the LED star ceiling panel is dimmer than the rest of the lounge, giving it a more subtle and relaxing feel. Two large classical paintings of the Roman Empire in rose gold picture frames hang on the black walls of the VIP area above four long, red leather Louis Vuitton sofas. Two long, rectangular-shaped black wooden tables custom-made by Versace are placed in the middle of the VIP room. Each holds four buckets filled with ice and complimentary champagne bottles. Those on the VIP list mingle with the rest of the partygoers where the music meets the dance floor. It's a forty-foot by forty-foot hardwood section toward the back of the lounge and the lighting is a little brighter than the rest of the lounge so that those on the dance floor can see one another a little better. To add a bit of home and camaraderie to the joint, the walls are painted black and red with pictures of King and his crew partying in different countries that they have been to; right beside those pictures are autographed photos of ballplayers and rappers that made it out of Queensbridge, some of which are in attendance for the opening. The picture hall of fame was King's way of saying, *don't forget where you came from or where you're going.*

To the left of the bar is a red wall; a focal point that King dedicated to the fallen soldiers from his crew who had died on the streets. Some crews pour out liquor or get tattoos in homage to soldiers that have earned their stripes, but King preferred to show his respect through photos for all to see eternally. Tone and Mel pictures were tastefully hung on the wall in rose gold picture frames side by side. The words centered above the pictures in gold letters solidified his feelings for each of them: *Gone But Never Forgotten.*

The atmosphere in the lounge begins to heighten and it is clear that everyone is having a good time. Meanwhile Haze is in the back office trying to get details from Nando about a storage facility of theirs which was robbed earlier in the morning. It was a hard hit for the crew; ten million dollars of dope, four million dollars of cocaine and five million dollars of methamphetamine pills had been taken and Haze wanted explanations; quick, fast and in a hurry.

"UN...FUCKIN'...BELIEVABLE!" Haze said, leaning back in his leather chair and staring at Nando.

"I have no idea how they got the drop on us. My men dropped off the first part of the shipment at your warehouse and then headed to my location, which nobody knows about, to drop off the rest. I don't think that any of my men are to blame for this. It had to be a set up because they were rushed as soon as they got there. They were sitting ducks for an ambush. I lost some really loyal soldiers this morning; four of my men were killed. Three motherfuckers in ski masks with M16s got the jump on them, from what I'm told," he lets out a slight sigh and shakes his head toward Haze. "There's a snake in your crew, my man. You and King better find out who it is, and quick before it happens again and your own men start dropping like flies," Nando stated, observing Haze and his reaction.

Hiding his anger and showing no emotion, Haze gets up from his custom-made Hermes Oak wood desk and walks over to his closet. As he opens the doors of his custom-made Hermes wooden closet, the latest top of-the-line designer dress shirts, blazers, sweaters and jeans hang from the rod. A dozen sneakers by Balenciaga, Gucci and Retro Jordan's take up the top self; as a dozen Tom Ford hard-bottom shoes in different colors and styles are placed side by side at the bottom of the closet. Before speaking, Haze scans through the section which is the left side of the closet where the dress shirts are, and he pulls out and puts on a black and red, silk Versace button-down shirt from his collection. As the silk hits his back a sense of composure comes over him, calming him down from what he just heard.

"Well, you don't have to worry about that. King and I are going to find out who was behind it. I give you my word!" he said before turning back and looking at Nando with a smile on his face. "And once we do, there will be hell to pay; their families will be erased right along with them," he assured Nando as he buttoned up his shirt and admired the way he looked in the full-length, stand-alone wood mirror in the corner.

"I know y'all will. I have faith in that," Nando replied, getting up from his chair and putting on his blue blazer.

"What a way to end the year, huh? I hope losing that much money isn't an omen," Haze said, staring in the mirror at the scar across the right cheek of his face. He shook his head before pulling out a Lano Estate cigar. "But let's forget about that right now; it's New Year's Eve and there are a lot of people out there partying and enjoying themselves and King should be here any minute. So let's go have a good time tonight and get fucked up like how y'all do in Mexico. We'll take care of everything tomorrow," he said, putting his arm around Nando as they both laughed and walked out of the office.

"It's show time!" Agent Mackey said to the other agents in the apartment. They all watched on the surveillance monitor as a beige Maserati blasting the song, "No Ordinary Love" pulled up and parked in front of Black Roses Lounge.

Hopping out the driver's side wearing a beige sport's coat over a black, silk Versace shirt, black jeans and tan construction Timbs is King. His beautiful fiancé, Kia, steps out of the passenger side. She turns heads in a pair of black, Tom Ford Nappa leather laced-up pumps, and a cream-colored short cut Givenchy dress that shows off her long legs and amazing curves.

We're finally gonna get you, you son of a bitch, Agent Bauer said to himself as he watched King and Kia walk into the lounge.

As they enter, all eyes are on them as they make their way through and begin greeting everybody that came to celebrate the New Year and the grand opening. Haze, coming from around the bar, walks up to King, hugs him and gives him a bottle of Dom Perignon. The two men fist bump and Haze instructs the DJ to turn off the music.

Heads turn in their direction and conversations begin to cease as Haze begins to speak.

"Everybody…please let me have your attention. I want to make a toast, so will everyone lift your bottles and glasses and let's toast to the newly-engaged couple: King and Kia. Congratulations to you both," Haze says as the lounge erupts in cheers and clapping that can be heard down the block.

"Good looking out, my nigga." King said, giving him a hug and then cracking a smile. "I see Hoffa's here, where's Gotti, is he coming through?" King asked, knowing that Gotti was parked across the street in the black S-Class Benz.

"Yeah, I just talked to him a couple a minutes ago, he's on his way."

"King…congratulations, my man," Nando said giving him a hug. "And this must be the beautiful wife to be. King, you're a very lucky man I tell you," he says as he kisses Kia's hand.

"What the hell are you doing here? I didn't think you were coming," King asked.

"I wasn't gonna miss your party, Felix is here too. He's over there in the VIP, fucking with some drunk ass bitch."

"I'm glad y'all came."

The excitement in the lounge grows as the time approaches one minute until midnight and everybody starts counting down; watching the TVs and anticipating the ball to drop in Times Square. King, Kia and S, stand next to each other at the bar with smiles on their faces.

"5, 4, 3, 2, 1. Happy New Year!"

Everyone in the lounge screams out loud at the top of their lungs, hugging and toasting to the New Year. The sounds of bottles popping are all over the lounge and smiles are on everyone's face except King, S, Haze and Hoffa.

King observes the lounge and notices Haze looking impatient and irritated as he talks to Hoffa in the VIP area. He calls them over, and S walks off toward his three shooters who are laying in the cut.

"Happy New Year! What the fuck is up, y'all wasn't gonna come over?" King asked with a smile on his face as he gives them both hugs.

"Yeah, he was telling me something I didn't wanna hear right now; that's all," Haze replied, lifting his bottle in the air as the three of them toast.

Across the street in the apartment the FBI were staked out in, the power went out shutting down all the equipment. All six agents inside the apartment pass out

266

from the Halothane sleeping gas that came through the ventilation ducks of the apartment. King knew that the FBI was staked out in the apartment and that they were going to be there tonight, so he had the power line to the apartment hit, the Halothane was on a timer placed in the ventilation system, and the front and back doors of the building locked from the outside. The three squad cars on duty from the local precinct four blocks away, along with the Fire Department's two trucks were called away to a fire in a warehouse on Borden Avenue that King recently purchased and had set a blaze, a half mile away from the lounge.

Hugging her fiancé and kissing him passionately on the lips, Kia stares into King's eyes knowing there might be a chance he won't come home alive. She whispers in his ear, "Kill this bastard and make it home; me and your daughter will be waiting for you," then she walks to the back of the lounge to a hidden door behind the mirror that leads into the apartment building in back of the lounge.

Watching her walk away, King's body fills with anger as he looks at S and nods his head as S and his shooters pull out their guns and place them beside their legs. Haze's three shooters (who are from Danny Boy's Skillman Avenue Crew) are dressed in black tuxedo's and they start to make their way to the bar from the VIP area.

Staring at the smirk on Haze's face, King takes a step back and looks out the front window and sees two black Tahoes pull up in front of the lounge. Five men hop out in blue windbreaker jackets with the letters *FBI* on the back of them and three of them rush the front door as the other two stay outside.

Walking in with their badges out, they walk through the crowd and straight to the bar and up to Haze. "Darren Hall, you are under arrest," the short and stocky Italian agent told him as his partner grabs Haze's arms and tries to place him under arrest.

"What the fuck are you talking about? Y'all ain't taking me anywhere! What's the charge and where's the warrant?" Haze demanded.

"Here's the warrant and you'll find out everything when we get to Federal Plaza. So don't make it hard on yourself and let's just go."

King watches as Haze is resisting arrest and Hoffa walks over to the door and takes a look up the block where Gotti is parked, moving his hand toward his waist. "Fuck it, plan B," King said to himself and into the ear piece as he pulls out his gun.

Looking out the window, Hoffa watches as a Ford pickup truck stops in the middle of the street behind Gotti's car and someone gets up from the back of the truck and on to one knee. Hoffa watches as the missile sent from the RPG destroys Gotti's car and engulfs it in flames, lighting up the block. Hoffa then pulls out his gun and screams out to Haze, "They're not Feds!"

Pandemonium erupts in the lounge as people start running toward the front and side doors. Shots are fired from the guns of Haze's shooters; killing two of the fake FBI agents as King fires off two shots missing Haze's head as he ducks behind the bar looking for the direction Haze had gone. People run past him screaming as multiple shots go off. King sees his cousin, S, and his shooters banging at Hoffa and Haze's shooters.

Shot after shot; all three of Haze's shooters bodies drop to the floor as S now focuses on Hoffa as he and his shooters chase after Hoffa out the front door.

Oh my God, S said to himself making it out the front door to the chaos taking place in the street. Hundreds of people run in different directions, scrambling to safety as the sound of the gun shots being fired overshadow the screaming.

Stepping over the dead bodies, King sees Haze sneaking toward the side door and sends two shots at him as Haze sends some back, running out the door.

"What the fuck?" Agent Bauer said, awaking to the loud sounds of the shots being fired in the street. Running to the window, he sees the gun battle going on in front of the lounge. Waking up the other agents, they all rush down the stairs but can't get out the front or back door.

"Cole, Smith, Crebbs…we need assistance; we're trapped in the building," Agent Bauer yelled over his walkie talkie to the other agents stationed outside; but he gets no response.

Emerging from the indented doorway of Maria's Spanish restaurant in all-black is Gotti; firing at S's shooters and killing two of them. King watches as Haze runs to his car, being covered by Hoffa who's shooting at S. *Fuck it*, King said to himself, sending four shots at Hoffa and forcing him to hide behind a car. As he makes it to the black Audi he had in place for himself down the block, he then drives after Haze's Porsche, down Vernon Boulevard heading toward Queensbridge.

"Sam, I'm at the side door; agent Cole and Smith died trying to get to the front," Agent Crebbs told him over the walkie talkie. Shooting the locks off of the side door and prying the door open with a crow bar, the six trapped agents rush out, guns in hand, and around the corner directly behind Hoffa.

"Behind you!" Gotti yelled out to Hoffa.

Without turning around, Hoffa aimed his gun behind him and fired off five shots at the agents, and one of them hits Agent Mackey directly in the forehead.

"Fuck!" Agent Bauer yelled as he and the other agents return fire and take cover behind the wall.

In clear view as Hoffa gets up and tries to run toward Gotti's direction, S tears him up from across the street; hitting him seven times and causing him to collapse before he could get to Gotti.

Gotcha, S said to himself, watching Hoffa fall.

Agent Bauer and the other agents come back from around the corner shooting in both Gotti and S's direction. Hitting Gotti in his stomach and legs, the shots aimed at S miss as he made it around the corner to his bulletproof Hummer. Lying on his back and without any hesitation or second thought, Gotti lifts his head off the ground and aims his gun at Agent Bauer as he approaches. But before he could pull the trigger, Agent Bauer put a bullet in his head and then stood over him and dumped two more bullets into his face. He turns around and walks back to Hoffa's body. "This is for Mackey, you son of a bitch!" Agent Bauer said standing over Hoffa. *Boom! Boom!* He fires two shots into Hoffa's head.

Turning right on to 41st Avenue from Vernon Boulevard, Haze notices in his rearview mirror a black Audi spinning the corner and gaining on him. "Fuck," Haze said, as he swerves, avoiding from hitting a kid running across the hill. Extending his left arm out the driver's side window, King lets off a shot, hitting the left back tire of Haze's Porsche and causing him to side swipe a couple of parked cars along the 41st side of 12th Street and then finally crashing into a car. Hopping out and firing three shots at King's car as he pulls up behind the Porsche, Haze runs around the corner and into the 41st side of 12th Street.

King reloads his gun and hops out and chases Haze into the block. The loud sound of King's Sig Sauer ringing off makes the youngins on the block run to the garbage cans where their guns are stashed. Passing the card tables and running through the basketball court, Haze fires three shots without looking at King. Dropping to one knee in the middle of the basketball court, King fires four shots back at Haze as two of them hit him; one in the lower back and one in the leg.

"It's Haze, he's being shot," a youngin' said to Fatal as Haze limps over to them and drops to the ground.

"Shoot that motherfucker!" Haze demanded Fatal and the youngins. The three youngin's, unaware of who's approaching them, lift their guns up and aim them at King as he walks toward them.

"Hold on…don't shoot homies; don't shoot. That's King," Fatal said to the youngins.

"What the fuck you mean *don't shoot*? I told y'all to kill that nigga! He don't run shit no more; he ratted, so he's food out here," Haze told the youngins and Fatal as King walks up to him and kicks the gun out of hand as he tried to aim at him.

"What the fuck you mean *I don't run shit,* nigga!" King said as he kicked Haze in the face, breaking his jaw.

Watching the anger coming from King toward Haze, Fatal knew what Haze told him wasn't true. "King, I knew this nigga was lying when he said you ratted and got the hood swept. That shit didn't sound right when he first told it to me," Fatal said as he takes a gun from one of the youngins. "Hann," he said, giving King his Mercedes Benz car key, the same one King had given to him a year ago as a birthday present. "Take my car and get out of here. It's parked right there at the entrance; it's the black Benz you gave me. We'll finish this nigga off for you."

Giving Fatal the key to his Audi and telling him where to take it, King kneels down and stares Haze in his eyes. "Look at you nigga, you could never, ever fuck with me in this street shit. Not you, not Hoffa, and not Gotti. Never!!!! And tell Mac I'mma kill him again when I get there."

Getting up and jogging toward the entrance of the block, the sound of multiple shots ringing through the air brings a smile to King's face and the feeling of satisfaction, as Fatal and the youngins dumped eighteen shots into Haze's face and chest.

Over thirty squad cars and multiple EMS and Fire trucks are on the scene in front of Black Roses Lounge. The carnage left on the streets and inside the lounge has every news crew from all the major news stations in New York reporting live from the scene.

"Haze was just killed on the 41st side of 12th Street," Agent Crebbs informed Agent Bauer who was leaning up against the trunk of a squad car, staring at all the news crews filming all the bodies covered by white sheets laying in the street on the sidewalk and in the lounge.

"This motherfucker just...Jesus Christ!" Lost for words and still in shock from watching his partner and best friend Agent Mackey get killed in front of him, emotion overwhelms Agent Bauer. He drops his head and tears start to fall down his face.

Driving on the open road of the Long Island Expressway with the top down, the cold air never felt so good to King as his left arm hangs out the driver's side window holding a cigar. Twenty minutes away from the safe house where Kia, S and the rest of S's crew are waiting for him to show up, a tear rolls down King's face as the images of Nicole and Kia's faces flash in his mind and thoughts of how much shit he put the two most important people in the world to him through.

What kind of shit this nigga got in the car, he thought as he scanned through the play list. "There we go, my nigga," he said as he put on a song named, "Where the Streets Have No Name" as a smile stretches across his face and the church organ strings play through the speakers. He exhales the cigar smoke in air.

*****

I'm Emily Halston and this is a Channel 5 breaking news report. We're sorry to interrupt your regular scheduled broadcast on this New Year's morning. It's 3:00 a.m. and it's January 1, 2013, and already we start the New Year off with a horrific story, which is the blood bath that took place in Long Island City, Queens. It all unfolded on

Vernon Boulevard, between 47th and 48th Avenue in front of the Black Roses Lounge. Thirteen people have been murdered, and three of them were FBI agents. We just got word that a car was blown up by a RPG grenade launcher. The NYPD has released a photo of the man you see on your screen now. He's the owner of the Black Roses Lounge; his name is Aaron Johnson, aka King. He's wanted for questioning by the NYPD in regard to a couple of the murders at the lounge. We head out now to Bill Russell who's reporting live from the scene.

The End

Acknowledgements

Special thanks to GOD up above who put me in a situation in which I utilized my time wisely and started to write this book. To Lorraine Elzia for taking the time out of your busy schedule to even read the rough draft of the book, to then editing my book. I cannot thank you enough. To Tyler Johnson for publishing my book. To Tiffany Hines of Giftedone Productions for creating the cover design of the book. Last but not least to my family and friends that believed in me and stood by me during trying times and still remain. I don't have to mention any names, you know who you are.

About the Author

Lee A. Pitts was born in the big city of dreams, New York City. Raised in the infamous Queensbridge projects, he grew up around different types of personalities and had a front row seat to what life was like in the ghetto.

His passion for writing all started at a young age when he would be in his grandparent's apartment, which was on the same block and two buildings over from his. It was there where he would watch his uncle write music and also watch his grandfather sit behind a old fashioned typewriter and type up his novels.

He began his creative career in 2003 when he started producing music for up and coming hip-hop artists who were from his neighborhood. The artistic feeling he got from producing them lead him to writing music lyrics and movie scripts. After years of applying his creative and artistic talents into music, he applied those same talents into the literary world. His first novel, Paint the City Red, was published in 2016.